OPHELIA ADRIFT

HELEN GOLTZ

For Mark, my brother

Adrift: broken loose from the moorings
From A Dictionary of Sea-Terms

CHAPTER 1

OPHELIA

One minute I felt numb, the next I felt scared ... I wish I could just feel numb permanently. I can see another train station coming into view; sometimes the signs go by before I can work out if it is the one I want. *Warrnambool.* This is it. It's just like Uncle Sebastian had said—large, red brick and around it green hills and homes in the distance. So quiet compared to the main railway station at home.

I could stay on the train forever, just keep going, riding this carriage until I am old and die. But I've resigned myself to my fate.

There he is. That must be him. I grabbed my book and pulled out the small photo I had pressed between the cover and the back page. It was an old photo of my mother with her brother, Uncle Sebastian. Yes, that was him, I think. He might be handsome if he lost the large black rim glasses he wore in the photo and still wore by the looks of it.

I waited until the train had completely stopped ... delaying the inevitable, and then I was out of time ... I had to get off. I reached up and grabbed my red suitcase from the rack above; my hands were shaking, crazy. I took a deep breath and checked out Uncle Sebastian again. He looked nervous too, and a little bit like Mum. I felt a bit sorry for him as he stood with his hands shoved in the pockets of a long black, wool coat, rocking back and forward. His black and grey streaked hair was windblown but there seemed to be a fair mop of it; wild hair ran in the family. I bet he's not that excited about having an orphaned niece show up on his doorstep cramping his style.

I took another deep breath and waited for the last two passengers in the carriage to pass me towards the exit. Pain ... just a wave of homesickness ... if only I was a few years older, I could have stayed in our home ... I could have looked after myself. Go, I coached myself. I walked towards the exit, stepped from the train carriage onto the platform and looked over at Uncle Sebastian. He was gone.

I don't know anyone here... what do I do, just get back on the train and go ... where? Now I was panicking!

I found him; breathe again. But Uncle Sebastian was walking away arm-in-arm with some other woman. I was about to call after him when someone grabbed my arm.

JACK

There's one thing I don't like about Ophelia Montague—she likes her feet firmly planted on the ground. She likes the solid feeling that it won't move or sway beneath her, it gives her comfort, yet she comes to me, to a seaside town where the ocean beats upon the shore and shipwrecks hide below its depths. Where I live.

I knew she was coming; I had the power to feel her presence long before she arrived. I'm not psychic, I'm ... well, I'm her soul mate. She's beautiful ... blue eyes, long dark and wild hair, and skin that said she was from the city. I had been waiting a long time for her to arrive.

Ophelia didn't see me, but I watched her and studied her

reflection in the train window. She looked haunted; her blue eyes too large for her face as though the shock had set them permanently round and her skin was a pale as ice.

She had not torn her gaze from the train window for hours, studying every town, checking the signs and now she was seeing for the first time the town of Warrnambool as it came into view. When the train began to slow down I felt her heart rate sore. I breathed her in; I want to hold and protect her and one day I would.

Her uncle was there to collect her; he would take her by car to our home town, to Port Fairy, just short of thirty kilometres away. I watched as she wheeled around in fright, squinting as she looked up into the sun at a tall stranger holding her arm.

"Sorry, I'm late, Ophelia, I can't blame the traffic, there is none, but I've always run late, your mother used to say I'd be late for my own funeral, but that's not the best thing to say at this time is it? I don't know why I said that!" Sebastian stumbled on. "My you are a young woman ... last time I saw you, you must have been eight, yes it was your eighth birthday and you insisted we call you Princess Lia, remember? But you are here now, that's wonderful, did you have a good trip? Let's get your bag."

Sebastian reached for her suitcase drawing a breath for the first time. Then he stopped to look at her.

"You look like your mother."

Ophelia smiled, it was the first time I had seen her smile in the whole month I had been studying her. "Hello Uncle Sebastian. I remember you now," she said.

Sebastian grinned; he looked pleased and kind of embarrassed, running his hand through his hair. He pushed his thin, silver-framed glasses further up his nose.

"I'm sure I haven't changed," he shrugged. "There's a big difference between eight and sixteen-years-of-age, but not much difference between thirty-five and forty-three except some grey hairs and maybe some weight gain—have I put on weight? Yes I'm sure I have. Come then, let's go home. Well to my home, your home now too. I hope you will make it your home, Lia, you are welcome, very welcome. Do you still call yourself Lia? It's much easier than saying Ophelia."

I saw tears well in her impossibly huge eyes and she smiled at him.

'Lia is fine, and I'll call you Uncle Seb instead of Sebastian then?"

"Indeed yes or just Seb," he agreed. "Of course you'll meet Adam tonight, he couldn't come to meet you, he's at work. I did tell you about Adam, didn't I? He's a boarder; his parents are nomads ... took off as soon as he finished school."

Sebastian turned and walked towards the footpath where three cars were parked: a sporty little dark green Jaguar, a red 4WD and an old cream-coloured Rover. Ophelia blinked away her tears and headed towards the Rover; it looked like the type of car her uncle would drive, I would have put my money on that one too. But instead, he went to the red 4WD. Ophelia's eyes lit up and Sebastian noticed.

He laughed. "You thought I was in the dodgy Rover, did you? Well, you would be right normally, but this is a company car, a tax benefit," he shrugged and opened the door for her. Ophelia slid in and waited as Sebastian put the suitcase in the back and slid into the driver's side. "I'm on the road a bit with my work; I have to drive to the surrounding areas and often inland. Plus, the dogs like to get in the back. I love dogs. Do you like dogs? I have two, Argo and Agnes, from the same litter. They run the house really; Adam and I are just allowed to stay with them."

"I like their names," Ophelia got a word in.

"They're named after ships, of course. The *Argo* was a 17-ton wooden cutter actually built in Port Fairy where we're heading, but it was wrecked on Portland beach in a storm in 1883. We'll go visit Portland, it's not far. The *Agnes* or as it was actually called the *Margaret and Agnes*, arrived in Portland Bay in 1852 when it was blown ashore. It lost all its cargo—potatoes, flour and bran. Imagine all that coming to shore or sinking?" He shook his head. " There are lots of shipwrecks in the area, that's why I'm here, of course,"

Sebastian looked towards Ophelia, before pulling away from the curb.

Sebastian talked way too much, not surprising he was a bachelor.

"Your mother said I talk too much," he said as if reading my thoughts. *You think?*

"Being a researcher I don't talk to many people with my work, sometimes none all week—not one— unless I'm getting groceries or the petrol, so she used to say that I use up as many words as I can when I meet a person," he stopped for breath. "The point of that story is that you must butt in if you want to get a word in because I'm not sure if I'll run out of words or if I'll talk like this always."

Ophelia smiled and then she began to laugh. A smile and a laugh in one day, things were looking up. Sebastian turned towards her and grinned, then her laugh became infectious and they both laughed until tears ran down their cheeks.

Ophelia was crying for her mother and father, and for new beginnings.

I couldn't wait until she met me—that would change her life, for the better.

CHAPTER 2

OPHELIA

I was lucky I guess, it was a pretty area. Along the way, Uncle Seb kept pointing sites out to me. So many green pastures, filled with black and white cows grazing that resembled the small ones that were in the toy farm sets. On the top of the rises were the occasional farm homes drinking in the ocean views. We came into Port Fairy itself; the little seaside cottages were sweet, some were timber like my home—my former home—and others were stone that Uncle Seb called bluestone. We drove through the town and I spotted a little house just like my old home—timber with a bullnose veranda. It looked as though a strong gale from the ocean would topple it, but the bluestone houses with their iron lacework were solid, there to stay.

Uncle Seb drummed his hands on the steering wheel; I think he was more nervous of me than I was of him, moving city, State and leaving my friends behind. All I wanted to see was his house, my new home. We drove towards the ocean.

"Almost there," he said reading my mind. "In fact you can see it now in the distance." He leaned down, looked through the windscreen, and pointed up the road to the top of a rise. "There she is".

"Seriously?" I breathed out.

He gave me a concerned look trying to read if I was enthusiastic about the house or freaking out. It stood alone on the horizon—in front of it, the ocean curled in-and-out, beating on the rocks that framed either side of the house. Further up the road was a smattering of houses. The road to it was winding but the house stuck out from its neighbours.

"That one there? On the rise?" I asked him.

"Yep, that one there. The only one there," he smiled with a glance in my direction. He steered the car along the winding road; the house falling in and out of sight.

"It's … amazing. Will it blow off or wash away in a gale?"

Uncle Seb laughed. "It hasn't yet, although there was one time I had to evacuate. She's a beauty isn't she? Been in our family for many, many years, otherwise I wouldn't be able to afford a house and land with ocean views here, these days. But when my great grandfather bought it—our great grandfather, although you get one extra 'great' I believe being a younger generation. Anyway when he bought it this area was not as trendy as it is now of course."

"Trendy?" I turned to face Uncle Seb. Maybe, just maybe, I hadn't come from the city to the backwater.

"Yep. Only three hours from Melbourne and the place has been taken over by city dwellers who want to escape here for a weekend. It's packed in summer." He shook his head as though the world was moving too fast for him. "Did I tell you we've got Wi-Fi at home? I work from the home office a lot, so it might look like a sleepy little town to a city girl, but everything is wired and reachable … if you want it to be."

Things were looking up. Uncle Seb's voice dropped. "I love the house; she has a bit of a sad story attached to her, I'll tell you one day, but she looks after me, Argo and Agnes. Of course Adam is rarely there—he starts work early and wanders in for dinner at dusk. But if you are lonely, you can borrow the car anytime you like, I don't go out that often for work, just down to the maritime museum, the one in Warrnambool, but when I do have to go out for work, I'm often away for a few days at a time."

"I don't have my licence, yet, I'm not old enough to drive." I think Uncle Seb might be truly clueless about teenagers.

"Really?" Sebastian frowned. "I must be thinking of France where they drive really young. Oh well, you can take the bus or train to Melbourne and there's a push bike in the shed for getting around locally. Plus the bus goes right past the bottom of the driveway if you wait near the letterbox and wave it down. Wave early though—Reg, the driver is not as young as he used to be or perhaps he's just colour-blind and can't see you if you are wearing a red jumper against the red letterbox."

"Right, wave early," I repeated after him. I checked out Uncle Seb at close range. If he had a makeover he would scrub up okay. He was tall and handsome in a geeky sort of way. Mum always said he was eccentric but Dad was less flattering of Mum's side of the family —saying Uncle Sebastian was from a strange gene pool.

"Can I ask you a question?" I broached the subject of his love life. Might as well get it out there.

"Of course, anything," he said, taking another corner a bit too fast.

"Do you have a girlfriend or wife or boyfriend?" I thought I had better cover the whole range.

"Nope. None of those. I like women, but I don't really have time or seem to meet women," he said. "I'm not so big on people ... not you of course ... other people ... I've just never been one for the company of many," he steered the car along the long beachside road.

I nodded. "I get that. Mum and Dad ... they were party people; we never had an empty house. I'm okay with my own company."

I saw the house come closer in view now; huge and rambling. Along the top level were two huge panoramic windows and on the level below, a single door looked like a mouth—a house with a surprised expression. The timber boards were bare; paint may have once adorned them but the house was stripped by wind and salt air. The nearest house was behind and at the end of the road, where three small properties edged along the roadside.

"We're here," Uncle Seb said turning into a winding driveway.

As we neared the house, I could see two huge dogs sitting like statues on either side of the front door.

"Wow, they're huge!" I exclaimed.

Uncle Seb smiled like a proud parent. "They won't eat you. That's Argo and Agnes—Great Danes, a fine breed. They weigh about 65 kilograms each those two, much more than you, but they're a very gentle breed, and very loyal. Did you know that dogs resembling the Great Dane can be traced back to monuments in Egypt dating back to 3000 BC? The breed originated in Germany, lots of good things come out of Germany ... cars for one and ..." he stopped. "Sorry, I'm ranting again. You must pull me up. We should develop a codeword for that, for pulling me up. Anyway, I always leave the back door open for them, but they like to look at the sea. What word can you use to stop me raving ... I'll think on it."

The two dogs came alive, their massive tails wagging.

"Your welcoming party," Sebastian said. He pulled the car into one of the carports and cut the engine.

The dogs bounded towards him and he greeted them enthusiastically. "Now Agnes, Argo, allow me to introduce our new member of the household, this is Miss Ophelia Montague. You may call her Lia, I'm sure."

They approached me enthusiastically. I held out my hand to each dog, allowing them to inhale my scent and patted them hello. I looked up at the house and around.

This was going to be my new home.

JACK

I watched Ophelia and Sebastian as they stood outside the large house—two levels and an attic. She looked so tiny framed by Sebastian, the dogs and with the house towering above her. Her arrival went better than I thought; perhaps Sebastian's endless banter proved a good distraction. And then the house wailed.

She looked up, eyes wide with surprise if they could be any larger.

"That's the house welcoming you," Sebastian told her.

"It is wailing!" she exclaimed.

"It does howl, but with delight most times," Sebastian assured her. He turned, looked out to the ocean and inhaled. "Lovely."

I swear that man has saltwater in his veins.

Ophelia turned to look too and I saw it—she shuddered. It was going to make my job much harder. I tried to see it from her perspective: the ocean went for as far as the eye could see in front and on the sides of the house. It grew darker in colour quickly, showing off its depth and the waves crashed into the shore and rocks not far from their front door.

"I like the rocks," she said.

I stored that fact away.

"Me too, I love to climb amongst them," Sebastian said. "Be careful though, the tide can come in quickly and sweep you off. Your mother would be very pleased I remembered to give you that warning." He looked satisfied with himself.

"Have people died from being washed off the rocks?" Ophelia asked.

"Oh yes, many," he said, and gazed out to sea. He said nothing for close to a minute, the longest time he had stopped talking yet. And then he continued. "But the little rock pools can be delightful. In summer you can sit in some of the little wading pools and cool off. Now let me show you around," he said and grabbed her red suitcase from the car, heading inside with Ophelia and the dogs in pursuit.

I stayed behind as Sebastian began to show Ophelia her new home, her new life. I would have to teach her to love the sea—no easy task. First though, I had to choose the best time to meet her so my life could begin.

OPHELIA

"I hope you like your level," Uncle Seb said.

"My level?" I thought I had misheard him.

"Oh yes, unless you get lonely, but I assumed being a young woman you would want your own space and to have a friend or friends around eventually or to play a bit of music or just do whatever young people do these days ... twittering, internet, Facebook. Agnes likes to have her own places too that are off-limits to the boys, don't you Aggie?" he stroked the white Great Dane with the brown ears and speckles. She nodded in agreement. "She may share with you as you are both girls. You travel light for a female."

I looked at my red case. "I guess. I just ... I couldn't decide whether to bring a lot of memories or move on."

Sebastian nodded his understanding. "Adam was living upstairs but when we heard you were coming, he moved downstairs and took the other side of the house."

"Oh, sorry, is he cranky?" I asked.

"Not at all," Uncle Seb assured me. "He's not here much, besides he didn't want girl germs," he said with a wink. "Right then," he led the way to the front door, which wasn't locked, but required a good shove to open.

"The salt air," he explained. "Some days the windows and doors open easily, other days they don't. Don't take it personally; I know the house is happy to have another woman present."

I laughed at the notion and then began to wonder ... Dad always said Uncle Seb was eccentric, downright weird really. I followed him inside, Argo and Agnes trailed behind and the door closed itself. Must be a breeze somewhere.

I couldn't believe the size of Uncle Seb's house as I wandered through; it was enormous and sparse. It was weird but it did feel like a person—a female—and I felt kind of protected inside her. In the entranceway prisms of light danced around the floor from stained glass porthole windows in the ceiling.

"I love this," I told Uncle Seb and turned in circles following the lights.

The two dogs followed me around as I twirled and Uncle Seb grinned at the sight of the three of us in a circle dance.

"Come, we'll have a tour," he said, and removed his coat, taking mine as well and hanging them on a coat rack near the door.

In front of the entrance hallway where we stood, a huge timber staircase ran up the middle of the room. Uncle Seb moved to it and placed my red suitcase on the bottom step.

To the left was a large living room with endless ocean views and a kitchen behind it. The living room featured a large iron fireplace in the corner with an equally large rug and two couches, one on each side. His and her couches—Uncle Seb and I might never see each other.

"The living area," he pointed to the area left of where we stood, then continued through the living room to the open plan kitchen which looked a bit like the galley on a ship—completely white or faded white now, bits and pieces hung from the ceiling, the benches were bare and not a bowl, a piece of fruit or a plate to be seen.

"Kitchen," he announced.

Sebastian strode back out of the kitchen, through the living room and then crossed the hallway to the room at the front of the house on the right.

"My office," he announced.

"Oh my." I stopped dead in the doorway. It too had doors opening onto the front timber deck and a stunning ocean view. It seemed every room and window did. Two long tables took pride of place in the centre of the room and a wide shelf ran around the room at desk height. On every spare surface, a model ship stood—old ships, modern ships, large and small ships, ships with sails, with steam engines and bits and pieces of model ships. The walls were adorned with drawings and paintings of ships and a bench stood near the window where a ship was currently being built.

"Ah yes, it's my passion. Some might say obsession, but I love the history. They are all accurate models you know. One day if you are interested, I'll introduce you to them all," Uncle Seb said.

It made sense that Uncle Seb positioned his office here rather than have his bedroom at the front; he worked from home most of the time and his work was all about ships.

"Right, now for our bedrooms," he said and showing incredible restraint he turned away from his office and moved out into the hallway again. I had to take two steps for every one of his. I caught up and followed as Uncle Seb walked under the staircase towards the back of the house, pushing open a door on the left and a door on the right as he walked. I glanced in each room; they were enormous and had huge windows that looked further up the coast with endless water views from both sides of the house. In each room, a king-size bed featured along with a couch and still, there was room to move.

"Adam has the left of the house and I am right, but not all the time," he laughed at his own joke.

The bedroom on the left was a mess. I grinned and looked to the right, it was orderly.

"Mm," I said. "Makes sense."

Uncle Seb laughed. Both Adam and Uncle Seb's rooms had doors that opened onto the back deck. Under the stairs was a specially designed dog bedroom, open but cosy.

"This is Agnes and Argo's room. They have their own doggy door," Uncle Seb said.

I looked at the doggy door in the back door frame; it was huge—I could fit through it with only slightly ducking my head.

Uncle Seb looked sheepish. "I guess it is more of a people door and wouldn't stop anyone breaking in, but we don't have much here worth breaking in to steal," he shrugged.

"I think someone would be very brave to break into a house with two huge guard dogs," I said and stepped away from Argo and Agnes's room. "Well Argo and Agnes," I addressed the dogs, "I must say you are neater than Adam and Uncle Seb."

The two dogs appreciated my comment and Uncle Seb nodded his head in agreement. Each dog had a large dog bed suspended about one foot off the ground by sea ropes and a view from the hallway to the deck and park area behind.

"They'll move beside the fire in the living room in winter of course and sleep on the rug."

"Of course," I agreed thinking of the homeless back in my city who would love to share Argo and Agnes's bed.

Uncle Seb took off again towards the front of the house. I chased after him.

"I have no secrets, so you are welcome on my side of course, if you can find anything to interest you there," he joked. "Adam might be more territorial. Now for your level."

He returned to the staircase, grabbed my suitcase and headed up to the next level. Argo, Agnes and I followed him upwards. I grabbed the timber rail, turned at the top of the stairs on arrival and looked back down. It was a large home but it felt cosy. I turned to find Uncle Seb smiling, waiting for me.

"Uncle Seb, I don't need a whole level really. I'm sorry," I said. He looked surprised.

"What for?"

"I feel like I've displaced you both. You have your life and now you have me ... this obligation," my eyes began to fill even though I tried not to cry and I blinked them clear as quickly as I could.

"Never an obligation, Lia, never. It's my pleasure to have you," he stumbled with words, "a pleasure and a privilege to have you here." I don't think Uncle Seb has had to express his emotions very often and his sincerity brought my tears closer to the surface. I breathed in deep to get control, smiled my thanks and he hurriedly continued the tour. The upstairs area was equally enormous with high ceilings and included a narrow staircase that lead to an attic. The house was clearly divided on each side of the staircase.

I stopped dead in my tracks and gasped. The entire front wall featured the two large glass panoramic windows that had looked like eyes from afar and through these you could see the ocean until it fell away off the edge of the earth. Uncle Seb stopped beside me and put down the suitcase. He looked out at the ocean.

"I forget sometimes how beautiful it is," he said. "I have to remember to look up and admire it." He sighed and turned away. "Now, the right side is empty ... guest rooms, spare rooms, whatever we like," he swung doors open. "A bedroom ... and ..." he walked down the hall beside the staircase, "bathroom ... and ... a storage area. I'm a bit of a hoarder."

I followed. "Wow," all the rooms had the most amazing views.

"But you, Lia, you own the left-hand side and the whole floor really." He returned, collected my case from where he left it and pushed it into a bedroom. "Here's your room, your bathroom and a spare room that you can use as you see fit, maybe a guest room for a friend from your old school or a new friend or a study room for school? All the furniture is new—Mrs Duxom went shopping and ordered it all. She chose white, everything white, even the quilt. She said you could add colour then, any colour you like. She did sneak a little pink in, but if you don't like it or want to change it ..."

Checking out the left side—my side—I wandered from the bedroom to the spare room to the bathroom and back to the bedroom with my mouth open. It was wonderful—big high ceilings, antique chandeliers with glass and pink crystal drops, the whitest of walls, timber floors and pale cream rugs, a welcoming plush quilt and plump white and pink pillows—it felt so plush like I had entered a room out of Vogue Living magazine.

I turned to Uncle Seb. "Thank you, I love it. You've gone to so much trouble."

"Never too much trouble for my only niece," he said and I could tell he was happy with my reaction. He looked away and back at me again with delight.

I wandered through the rooms again as he watched, swaying on his heels, his hands in his pockets. The bathroom had a huge cast iron bath all new and polished and the view from the window was unbelievable. I could watch ships on the horizon while I'm bathing. I went back to the spare room with the desk and double bed and back to my own bedroom with a four-poster double bed and the white netting all around it.

"It is beautiful, dreamy, thank you," I circled the bed and ran my hand along the white netting.

Sebastian nodded and reddened with pleasure. Argo and Agnes sat on either side of the door looking like ancient protectors of the room.

"More to see," he said leading the way outside the room to the small stairs that led up to the attic.

"And that," he looked skyward, "is our viewing room. Most mornings we all go up—that is me, Argo and Agnes—and I take a coffee and sit to look at the ocean. Plus if we sight a ship at any time of the day we all meet there," he said including the dogs in his glance. "It is rather lovely. Come see."

The way Uncle Seb spoke I could see the dogs and the house were his family. The dogs raced ahead up the attic stairs and I followed them and Uncle Seb. Two large chairs sat in front of the windows and looked straight out to the ocean. With the height there was no sense of being on land, it was as though the attic floated in the ocean. The dogs wandered along the large windows.

I'm sure my jaw dropped open and Uncle Seb grinned with pleasure as he showed off his prize old home.

"She's something alright," he nodded. "Well, that's the house," he began the descent down to the bedroom level again with the dogs following behind. He stopped before descending to the lower level and turned to face me.

"Now, Mrs Duck—her name is actually Mrs Duxom but we call her Mrs Duck, don't know why, it just stuck—anyway Mrs Duck comes every weekday after twelve to clean, wash and cook dinner, she's been with me for over a decade now. On the weekends, we fend for ourselves! You'll meet her soon enough. I will go put the kettle on for tea. Take your time, Lia."

I thanked Uncle Seb and watched him take the stairs at a gallop down to the lower level, Argo beat him down, Agnes stayed with me.

My room was beautiful, dreamy even—but I felt bad for liking it, as though I was being traitorous to Mum and Dad. I moved to the window and looked out over the ocean. An incredible feeling of loneliness swept over me and I grabbed my chest; I don't know why, I knew that wouldn't help. As if reading my emotions, Agnes moved closer to me and I stroked her head.

The sun would soon set across the ocean; the shadows were already long across the rocks. Then I saw movement at the base of the rock ... a person, a man with fair hair? I turned back but there was no one there.

JACK

She saw me, just a hint of me but I was gone before she looked back ... it is safer that way for a while, well, until we're officially introduced. I can't believe she's here at last; I feel like I have waited forever for this moment in time. So I can wait and do it properly ... let her discover me.

Not everyone is happy she's here, there are petty jealousies rising ... a fear that she will replace all others, receive all my affection, and take up all the room I have in my heart. They have grounds to be worried.

~

OPHELIA

I woke with a fright, I could hear yelling, and just for a few seconds, I didn't know where I was. It was Uncle Seb yelling. I can't believe I slept, morning caught me by surprise—I haven't slept so heavily ... well, since Mum and Dad died.

Uncle Seb was pounding up the stairs. I threw off the covers, shoved my feet into my Ugg slippers, chucked my dressing gown around me and ran towards the door. Uncle Seb nearly collected me as they ran past. He thudded up the stairs with Argo and Agnes in pursuit. Somehow Uncle Seb was charging along while balancing two cups of tea!

"Morning, Lia, there's a ship, come on," he called as he headed up the attic stairs; the dogs took them in two bounds.

Ship! All this racket for a ship, really? I glanced to the large, solid brass ship clock in the hallway. *5.35am, good grief.* Uncle Seb called out again. I sighed and went to the attic stairs and climbed up finding all three of them looking out the large windows.

"Morning, here you are," Uncle Seb handed over a hot mug of tea as I sunk into the seat next to him. He wore a loose grey T-shirt and track pants; his hair was bed hair at its best. I reached down and gave Argo and Agnes a morning pat each as they lowered themselves at our feet, facing the ocean.

Ahead, through the floor-to-ceiling windows was the most

amazing view ever—a full panorama of the ocean and centre place, crossing the front was a large ship.

"Oh wow, it looks like it is in our front garden," I blinked to wake up properly and gazed at it through the steam of my hot tea. "I didn't think it would be that amazing."

Uncle Seb grinned. "Worth getting up for after all?" he ribbed me.

I shrugged and smiled. "Yeah maybe."

"It is something, isn't it? We never tire of watching them," he said including the dogs who also looked out to sea.

"Where's Adam?" I asked.

"He's out having a run. He does most mornings."

I nodded, pleased that the first time I met him I wouldn't have bed hair. Adam didn't come home for dinner last night, for my first night, but I heard a car arriving and the door opening just after ten or so. The house had moaned as well, a welcome home moan I suppose. I wasn't in a hurry to meet more people.

We watched the ship moving slowly across the horizon.

"I don't get how they float … I mean I know the science of how they float," I added quickly before Uncle Seb started his lecture on the ship's buoyancy properties. "I mean, I'm blown away by how they float."

He nodded. "We'll make a sea lover of you yet, Lia, you wait and see, won't we kids?"

Argo barked on cue, a deep bark that came from his big chest.

I leaned over and stroked his beautiful head.

"You should go down and walk around the shores, visit the maritime museum, you could even go on a tour to look at the wrecks," Uncle Seb suggested.

I shuddered. "Creepy."

"You think?" he asked. "I love them. So do the divers—the ships are a great reminder of our history."

"But didn't lots of sailors die? Awful to think that we enjoy the sights which once would have been the cause of a lot of grief," I said.

"I guess," Uncle Seb said, "but you could say that about a lot of history and sights. Besides not every ship had a full crew that perished. Like Agnes' ship ..."

Agnes' ears twitched on hearing her name.

"...it was a crop ship." Uncle Seb pointed straight ahead.

"And just there, the Essington, sank in 1852, she was carrying a cargo of coal."

"Why did it crash?" I asked.

"She began to take water and then ran ashore. Believe it or not, you can still get little bits of coal washed ashore after rough weather. Now that's creepy if you think about it," Uncle Seb said. "And there," he pointed to the left, "is where the Thistle went down. She was blown ashore on Christmas Day in 1837 and was carrying wattlebark, you know, stripped from trees?"

I shook my head, wattlebark was new to me, but I guess a lot of Uncle Seb's world was new to me. My day used to exist of getting up, checking my Facebook page, going to school, going to sport after school sometimes, homework and hanging with my parents and friends. This shipping world was totally foreign and this house was something else. Just as that thought crossed my mind, she softly moaned and rocked just a little with the shore breeze.

"But, the greatest mystery of them all," Uncle Seb continued, "was the Mahogany Ship. She went missing in 1836 and has never been found to this day, so she could be anywhere," he waved his arm.

I felt goosebumps rising on my skin. "How can a whole ship be lost and never found?"

"Yeah, sounds impossible, doesn't it?" Uncle Seb sipped his tea. "But it happens. Planes used to go missing in the Bermuda Triangle all the time, stranger things have happened. The Mahogany was sighted a few times, or people thought they sighted an ancient-looking wreck here and near Warrnambool, but she's never been found."

I looked over at my uncle and studied him. "Have you looked for it?"

"It's been part of my life's work. I can't stand not knowing where it is ... it has to be out there somewhere," he squinted. "The government even put up a reward once, $250,000, but no sight of it."

"Wow, that's weird." I looked back out to sea, watching the ship move along the horizon line.

"Do you believe there are ... ghosts, like sailors lost at sea trying to come to shore?" I hesitated to ask in case Uncle Seb thought I was a major idiot but curiosity got the better of me.

"Oh yes!" he said.

"Really? I thought since you're a scientist and kind of technical, that you would think that was stupid," I said.

"I think you have to be open to everything in the universe," Uncle Seb said and surprised me again. "There have been many ghostly sightings, not just of the Mahogany. I wish I could say I've seen some, but no, not in all the time I've lived and worked here. I want to see them ... but you'll find plenty in the village who will tell you stories. There are second and third generation ancestors of ship crews here, so lots of tales, some probably exaggerated along the way." He turned to look at me.

"Why, seen a ghost ship?"

"No," I laughed. "I've only been here a day! But ... yesterday at dusk, when you left me to settle in, I thought I saw something on the rocks, but when I looked back it was gone ... could have been just the light on the water, nothing, you know, but that's what got me thinking about the spirits of the sea."

"I like that," Uncle Seb said, "spirits of the sea."

We turned to view the ocean liner again and Uncle Seb pointed to the rocks. "There's Adam now ... see there, near the stage ..."

"Stage?" I squinted across the beach to the sand dunes.

"We, the locals call that rock outlet that looks like a stage, the stage."

I watched Adam as he walked onto the stage and stretched, finishing with his hands on his hips looking out to sea, his silhouette dark against the morning sky.

"How can you tell who it is from here?"

"I've known Adam since he was a baby. Besides, he goes there most mornings after his run. After a while, you get to know most of the people in the village. I can pick them by the way they walk and talk."

"How come he's staying with you if I'm allowed to ask?"

"Sure. When he finished high school last year, his parents wanted to travel but he got the apprenticeship. So he decided to stay and rather than flat alone, he moved in here," Uncle Seb said. "It's a big place and we don't see each other much."

"Your family is getting bigger and bigger," I said.

Uncle Seb looked over at me and smiled like the thought hadn't occurred to him.

"That's true," he said. "That's a good thing. Your world will be bigger too once you start school on Monday and make some new friends."

"Is it far?" I asked, 'to school I mean?" I finished my tea and thanked Uncle Seb.

"About twenty-five minutes on the school bus. You would be used to that in the city."

I nodded. I wasn't looking forward to it; I wanted to finish high school with my friends in Brisbane. Everyone here would already have their friends sorted.

The ship was moving out of the frame of the window. The dogs stirred and Agnes rose and put her head in Uncle Seb's lap. I turned as something caught my eye; it was just Adam as he jumped from the 'stage' and began to walk up the beach towards our house.

"Ask Adam to tell you about his ancestors, interesting story there," Uncle Seb said, rising. "Breakfast!" he declared and Argo and Agnes jumped up and took to the stairs. "Come down when you're ready. I'll scramble some eggs."

CHAPTER 3

OPHELIA

The school was huge; modern and crowded. A sea of blue uniforms filled the yard and with a deep breath and a wish to be anywhere but here, I threw my backpack over my shoulder and entered the school gate. What I would give to go back to my other life —to be walking into the grounds of my old school and catching up with everyone again after the holiday break.

Uncle Seb warned me it might take a while to fit in; he'd changed schools a few times when he was a kid with his and Mum's dad being in the Air Force. He offered to come with me, but I told him it's cool, I'm sixteen, not six and I would be fine. Besides, I have to learn to be alone now.

It started on the bus on the way in, I was the circus freak—no one spoke to me of course but they all seemed to know each other and I could see them staring and whispering. I guess a new girl arriving for year eleven is going to attract a bit of attention; especially arriving for term two after the school holidays. Worst case scenario, I only had half of year eleven and all of year twelve left ... I could just spend lunch hours in the library and do my own thing.

I sighed and told myself to get on with it. I followed the signs to the administration block and presented myself at the front desk.

"Now you are either Jacqui Passmore or Ophelia Montague and given Jacqui is going into grade four today, I'm guessing you are Ophelia?" a large red-haired woman, with a name tag reading *Mrs Carroll* said to me.

"I'm Ophelia Montague, with no desire to do grade four again!" I smiled at her.

Mrs Carroll laughed heartily. "You wait until you are my age dear, you would give it all to go back to grade four. Now, we have a buddy for you ... that is, a buddy system, someone who will look after you for your first week."

"Oh, that's good," I brightened.

"You didn't think we'd just throw you in class amongst that lot and let you fend for yourself did you? In fact, here she comes now."

I followed Mrs Carroll's gaze and turned to see a thin Asian girl walking towards the office. She wore wire-framed glasses and had a long dark braid of hair worn on one side of her head only. She wore the uniform to perfection—even her socks were pulled up to her knees. Pinned near her collar was a small badge that read *Prefect*.

"There you are, dear," Mrs Carroll greeted her. "Ophelia Montague, this is your buddy for the week, Peggy Carboney. Peggy is one of our top students and she'll look after you."

Peggy stuck out her hand and I shook it. "My name's Margaret, but really, how old fashioned, so I go by my nickname, Peggy, because I really like horses and my mother used to call me Pegasus."

Right, I tried to keep up.

Peggy turned. "Oh sorry Mrs Carroll, I hope your first name isn't Margaret?"

"Quite alright my dear, it is actually Carol. Carol Carroll, can you believe I married a man with the surname Carroll, I used to be Carol Dartmoor when I was your age." She laughed heartily. "But now, Ophelia is a lovely old-fashioned name."

"From Shakespeare," I added. "Thanks for looking out for me this week," I said to Peggy.

"My pleasure. We don't get many new people in year eleven, we get some in year seven moving over from other schools, but most of us went to primary school together. We've both got English for our first subject, so I'll introduce you around. Bye Mrs Carroll."

Peggy said all that in one breath and then she took off. I gave Mrs Carroll an appreciative wave and hurried to catch up with Peggy.

"I know what you are thinking ... how can I be Asian with a surname like Carboney," Peggy said.

The thought hadn't crossed my mind but I didn't have a chance to tell Peggy that because she kept talking.

"My mother is Malaysian but my father is Australian. They met when my father was working overseas; he's a violinist and so is my mother. They met performing. Romantic huh?"

"Sure," I agreed following Peggy. I didn't really like small talk ... once you got past the weather chat, it seemed kind of pointless, but I gave it a shot.

"So are you musical?" I asked her.

"Not a bit."

Well that went well.

"Must be exciting to be new in town and at a new school," Peggy continued, her eyes lit up. "I've been here all my life. Mum and Dad go away to perform sometimes, but we've always lived here. Are you excited?"

"No, not really," I said. "I've left behind my best friends and I'm guessing most people here have their own group by now ... so I feel a bit ..."

"On the outer?" Peggy finished as we walked into a hallway stacked with lockers.

"Exactly ... on the outer," I repeated.

She pointed me towards an empty locker. "Will that one do? You just need the English textbooks and a pad."

"Sure," I said and fished for my lock and key in the side of the backpack.

"Don't worry," Peggy grabbed a few books from the locker three-up from me. "I've been on the outer since day one, so I get it," she laughed. "You've always got me."

"Thank you," I smiled at her. "I appreciate it."

Peggy blushed; I don't think she was accustomed to praise. I'm glad I had her though—it would make entering the classroom easier.

"Let's go meet Mr Wall, our English teacher, you'll like him, he's funny." She waited as I locked up and then Peggy led the way.

Mr Wall stood at the front of the classroom and held a thin book to his chest. He was a small, skinny man with large, black-framed glasses, a full crop of dark hair and a big grin. I did a rough count; twenty-four students sat in the class.

"Okay, how many of you read *The Glass Menagerie* like you were supposed to over the holidays?" he asked.

There was a show of about a dozen hands.

"Hmm," he sighed. "There should only be one hand not up and that's our new person who didn't know she had to read it. Well those who haven't read it will be reading late tonight then, won't you? Any chance you have read it, Ophelia?"

"Ah yes, we did it last year," I answered.

He grinned. "Excellent, we have an expert in our midst. I would start paying Ophelia off now if you want help."

"But it's depressing, Sir," Rodney Brady quipped.

"Yes, Rodney, it is. But so is the Australian cricket team at the moment and that doesn't stop us playing cricket, does it? Now let's begin by looking at the lead characters, do we like them? Mr Jones?"

"No, Mr Wall."

"No indeed, they are not likeable," Mr Wall agreed. "Mr Smythe, stop staring at the new girl and look at me please!"

Everyone laughed and I felt everyone's eyes turn to me except Smythe's. I sunk down lower in the chair.

～

HOLLY

On our way home from school, I saw Ophelia—the new girl—at the bus stop. She was small, thin and pale with dark hair and big eyes ... sort of startled. I was about to say hi when the bus arrived so we all piled on.

I sat behind my brother; we don't want to sit together. "Sit here, if you like," he piped up as she passed; he would.

Ophelia turned towards him, I don't know if she recognised him from the English class earlier. He pointed to the empty seat beside him.

"Thanks," she dropped next to him.

"We're neighbours, sort of. I live at the end of the street, near the dead end and you're ... well perched on the edge. I'm Harry. Harry Geering."

"Ophelia ..."

"I know," he cut her off. "We all know your name—you're the only new person this year, but you'll find it harder to remember all of ours. How do you shorten that? Got a nickname?"

"Lia," Ophelia answered.

"Better," he agreed. "I get called Geers."

I couldn't help myself and I leaned forward and stuck my head between them.

"No one calls you Geers," I said and Harry rolled his eyes. I extended my hand to Ophelia. "I'm Holly."

"She's my twin sister," Harry said in a flat voice.

I smirked. "Ophelia can tell that I'm sure, except I'm clearly the better looking twin."

Ophelia laughed. "You look nothing alike," she looked from Harry to me. Harry had ginger hair and freckles with green eyes, while I was blonde, bleached blonde, with green eyes which I heavily traced in pencil because they popped like that.

"We looked alike when we were kids before Holly started ruining our natural given beauty," Harry said.

I ignored him and addressed myself to Ophelia. "You've come from Brisbane? I heard you're staying with Sebastian. He's lovely, our mum has a crush on him, but I don't think he's ever noticed, even though she's been dropping over meals and cakes since she and Dad divorced five years ago."

"Perhaps you can put in a good word for her," Harry added.

"But then, if they hitch up, we could all end up living in the one house," I pointed out the obvious. "That would be insane. How many bathrooms does your house have?"

"Three," Ophelia said.

I smiled, getting ahead of myself. "Three, well, that might work."

Ophelia laughed, I think we were going to like this new girl.

ADAM

I finished work early today and got home just after three. I hadn't met Sebastian's niece yet. She was in bed when I got home last night and she was still up in her room this morning when I had my shower and left for work. Poor kid, must be awful to have your world pulled out from underneath you. I changed out of my work gear and made my way down to the beach for a surf. The waves were crap, so I had a quick swim and then ventured onto the rocks so I could watch the tide come in. I took a deep breath; I loved the salt air.

As the last wave was sucked back out, I saw all the bubbles from the little pippis appear in the sand before the next wave returned to cover them. I licked the salt spray from my lips. One more month until it was officially winter and the warm air would be replaced with a chill and all the summer tans would fade. I brushed some sand off my arm looking at the tan I got this summer.

The water level began to rise—I moved higher to sit down onto a dry rock and rested my chin on my legs. The wind rose and whipped my hair into my eyes; it was thick with salt from my earlier swim. I glanced out imaging as I often did what it must have been like to row out in wild conditions in the dark to rescue someone like William, my great-times-by-three-grandfather did, especially when he couldn't swim. Don't think I'd do it, not really heroic I know but that's the way it is. You learn the strength of the ocean growing up with it and you gain a healthy respect for it if you're clever.

I heard a car and turned to see Seb driving along the nearby road heading home after work. I raised a hand in salute as Sebastian's arm extended, waving from the 4WD window. I followed his journey up the winding road to the ramshackled house perched on the edge that we call home. I saw her then, Ophelia, I hadn't seen her come home. She was standing framed in her bedroom window—a small figure, a silhouette, but it was her. I thought she was looking at me so I raised my hand and waved to her. She seemed to hesitate, like she didn't want to look like she had been looking at me, and then she waved back.

She move away from the window and I saw her pass the next level of windows as she made her way down, probably to greet her uncle.

I jumped as a wave licked my feet and brought me back to reality. The tide was coming in fast. I rose and scuttled off the rocks before it was too late.

Time to meet Ophelia in person.

CHAPTER 4

OPHELIA

"*E*xcellent," Uncle Seb exclaimed swallowing his last mouthful of Mrs Duck's beef stew.

"Delicious," I nodded my agreement and Uncle Seb smiled, pleased I had done my part in devouring it. It was a great beef stew. Sometimes I felt guilty that my appetite was returning.

"She can cook our Mrs Duck. She would make a good wife," Adam ribbed Uncle Seb who laughed and shook his head.

"Except she's married and twenty years older than me," Uncle Seb reminded him.

"Except for that," he agreed.

I had been trying to study Adam without staring. He was only two years older than me and had finished senior last year, but he seemed a lot older. He was easily a head taller than me, but slight and sporty. He had a runner's physique.

"It is inherited," Uncle Seb said.

"What is?" I asked, having lost the train of the conversation. I topped up everyone's tea from the pot in the middle of the table.

"Talking, it's inherited. Either that or you've caught it from me already."

I guess I had said more over dinner than I had probably said since I arrived a few days ago. I shrugged. "First day at school, I had a lot to tell you ... about Peggy the Prefect, and Harry, although he wants to be called Geers but Harry's easier to remember because he has a twin, Holly—Harry and Holly—but you probably knew that ... and then Mr Wall was fun, but I liked Mr Meadows too, he made history interesting. So there you have it." I could feel myself redden. I'm sure Adam thought I was a rambling idiot.

"My parents are rovers," he said, "so I've changed school six times."

I gasped. "That's awful."

"Yeah," he agreed. "Fine if you're an extrovert, but I'm not. So think of me as your big brother. If anyone hassles you, I've got your back."

"Thanks," I liked him already. "I've always wanted a brother or a sister."

"Yeah, I did too until I got one," he said.

Uncle Seb sat back and smiled watching the interaction between us. "I'm relieved that your first day went well, I was worried," he said.

"Thanks Uncle Seb." I was touched by his concern. "I thought I'd go for a walk on the rocks. I'll be back before it gets dark if I'm allowed?"

Uncle Seb rose, reached for my plate and Adam's and took them to the sink. "You are your own person now, Lia, I trust you."

"Want some company?" Adam asked.

"Sure," I shrugged casually. "Can we take the dogs Uncle Seb?"

"They would love that, Lia," he agreed.

"I'll just get a pullover," Adam said, leaving the room.

I grabbed my cup of tea, moved to the sink and reached for a tea towel as Uncle Seb filled the sink with hot sudsy water. He lowered his voice and turned to me. "You've had that sex talk haven't you?"

I choked on my mouthful of tea. "Uncle Seb!"

"I didn't say I was going to give it to you, but you know, I guess I have to check you know what happens you know when ...

"Yeah," I cut him off, "thanks I've got it under control."

He nodded, scraping off the plates. "Good. Do you need to go on the pill?"

"What! Really?"

"I don't know, Lia, I'm supposed to be responsible but I'm not really, well I'm very good at looking after the furry kids—they've been desexed, but that's a bit different. You have to tell me if you need me to organise something for you … you don't want to get pregnant … but Mrs Ducks can help you with that sort of thing."

I held up my hand willing him to stop talking now. "Uncle Seb, stop right there. I'm not going to get pregnant, I'm not even doing … you know what … and I have no intention of doing it at this point in time… and I can go to the doctor by myself if need be, but thanks for asking."

"Good, good," he exhaled and turned to the sink to wash up. "But you had better come grocery shopping with me, at least the first time or every time if you like, so I know what to get you each week … do you buy special girl products?"

"Grocery shopping we can conquer together," I assured him adding my teacup for washing.

He sighed with relief and placed a washed plate in the dish rack. I grabbed it and wiped.

"Thank goodness, that's over," he said. I've been thinking all day how to raise the topic."

"Really? Because you could have fooled me just blurting it out like that!" I teased him.

He grinned and looked a bit sheepish. "Well, everything else should be easy from now on."

Adam reappeared, with dog leads in hand, a pullover and the dogs sticking close.

"They knew before I grabbed the leads," Adam said.

"Yes, you've got to spell it not say it," Uncle Seb told us. "Forget the wiping, I'll do these. Go and hang around the rocks, look out for Neptune's necklaces."

"What are those?" I asked as I put the salt and pepper shakers back in the cupboard.

"It's green-coloured algae that can grow to thirty centimetres long and it has all these pieces joined together that look like a string of pearls only ..."

"It's a string of algae," I grimaced and flicked the towel at Uncle Seb before hanging it up. "See ya," I called and headed out the door behind Adam, Argo and Agnes, before he could go into more detail.

JACK

I had been watching her the last few days, mainly at night but she didn't see me. Although, she caught a glimpse of me on her first day. Now she was coming towards me, Adam beside her and the dogs running in circles around them. She took off her sandals and hitched her fingers through the straps. I saw her dig her toes into the sand; that lovely feeling when it is cold and moist—strangely good. She looked out to the ocean and inhaled the salty air, then glanced back conscious of the security of her new home behind her.

For a moment it was like she looked right at me, then turned to Adam. He was leaning over looking into a rock pond and pointing something out to her. They weren't comfortable together yet, but he seemed to be taking her under his wing. They looked like they could be brother and sister; she had the palest of blue eyes and his were almost the same colour as the deep blue of the ocean. His black hair was straight and long at the front; it kept flicking in his eyes. She reached for a band around her wrist and tied her own dark hair back as the wind whipped around them. I was near enough to hear them. The dogs sensed me and circled.

"Want to walk that way?" he nodded up the beach.

"Sure." Ophelia followed him as he turned and began to walk further up the beach towards the public swimming area and the surf lifesavers' building. He stopped and waited for her to walk beside him. The beach was empty except for the occasional seagull hovering above and the big limbed dogs lolling around them. I followed them too but they couldn't see me.

"So you know most of my teachers?" Ophelia said to him.

"Yeah," Adam said. "And I know a lot of the kids in your grade because the middle grades do sport and dances together."

"So what do you do now?" she asked.

"I'm an apprentice boat builder. The company I work for builds and fits-out boats and we do repairs too."

"That's kind of cool," Ophelia said. If she thought that was cool, wait until I introduced her to my world. She continued. "Uncle Seb loves his boats."

"Yeah doesn't he just," Adam smiled. "Don't get him started ... I've been trapped before."

Ophelia laughed.

Her laugh was almost musical; I could listen to that all day.

Adam continued. "I'm only working on the small stuff at the moment like jet skis and pleasure craft, nothing that would interest Seb, but I'll work my way up. Last year they had naval vessels to work on and I'd love to do that."

"Here?"

"No, we go to Williamstown for that, or sometimes Portland," he said. "Oh, you're not from around here ... that's still in this State; Portland is about an hour's drive from here and Williamstown about three-and-half hours by car."

"Right," she smiled at him. "I'm still not sure where I am now, but I'll get there." She looked out to the ocean. She felt a stabbing pain in her heart which I picked up on too. She was remembering that she didn't have a home anymore. I involuntarily touched my own heart; I knew what it was to be displaced.

"I'm sure you will find your way eventually," he smiled at her.

"You like the sea then?" Ophelia asked him.

"I love the sea. I couldn't imagine not being near it or seeing it every day. When summer comes, this beach will be filled with surfers, swimmers, and sun bakers," he looked over at her. "You surf?"

"No."

"Swim?"

"If I can touch the bottom," Ophelia blushed. "I'm not much of a fish." She wandered to the edge of a rock pool and looked at the small life inside it. Adam joined her and they climbed up higher. I wanted to show them the power of the ocean, test Adam a little to see if he would run or help her. This would show him up.

My rogue wave hit the rock with a roar and she fell back in fright. Adam grabbed her, helping her off the rock and onto the sand. He lowered her down.

"Sorry, that scared me," she righted herself, her hand on her heart.

"Yeah, it does that."

I wouldn't have let her come to any harm, it was just a test. Her heart was beating too fast.

"That could have sucked me out to sea!" she stared at the now calm water. "Where did that come from?"

Adam shook his head. "Beats me. But there are no rips there at the moment and I'm here, you wouldn't have been sucked out."

I saw her shudder and she moved further onto the sand away from the rocks. The dogs circled them again, Argo licked her hand reading her stress, and she ran her hand over his coat. It probably wasn't the smartest thing to do—creating that wave—chances were I've made her more scared of the sea now.

They continued their walk with the dogs in a blissful zone of fresh air and open space. I was trying to read Ophelia and Adam's body language; it wasn't flirting I felt between them, it was needier. If she liked him, she wouldn't fall for me and I would have to fix that. I know girls thought Adam Ferrier was handsome with his tan and athletic build—strong arms and chest, probably from his work. He looked fit. I was the complete opposite—girls have said I'm cheeky and boyish, they like my dimples and fair hair, yeah girls usually love that stuff. I returned to watching them.

"So how long will you be staying with Uncle Seb?" she asked.

Adam picked up a stick and threw it. Both dogs chased in pursuit.

"Not sure," he said. "As I mentioned, my parents were wanderers," he started. "Since I was born, we've been on the road, they're real nomads. But this is their base, they own a place here and always come back—sometimes it might not be for a couple of years. I've been home-schooled as well as started at six different schools. I begged them to just let me finish high school in one place. So when I got into year eleven, they agreed to stick around for the two years."

"That's tough," Ophelia said. "I miss my friends and everyone has been really kind, but they already have their groups."

"I know. A bit easier for guys because if you're okay at sport, you can at least hang out in a team. Anyway, the folks agreed to stay put until I finished school and they had their bags packed before my graduation dance," he laughed.

"So they left with your brother or sister?" Ophelia asked.

"Little sister. She's only eight—she was a 'surprise' baby."

"Don't you miss them?"

I could feel by his reaction that he did, but he wasn't going to show Ophelia his soft side.

Adam shrugged. "Sometimes. I could have gone with them, but it was a big deal getting the apprenticeship ... over two hundred applied. So I really wanted to do it rather than go on the road. They'll be back for Christmas and then head off again probably."

"How did you come by Uncle Seb though?"

"He and my dad met a few times at the Maritime Museum. They became a bit chummy and Seb helped me with my apprenticeship application. When Dad and Mum wanted to move on, they didn't want to leave me in the house or with flatmates in case we had too many parties," he grinned. "So they rented it out on a six-month lease and they just keep extending it if they're not ready to come back yet. Seb offered his place. He won't accept rent, but I put in for groceries and I try and do a bit around the house like mowing and repairs. Seb's not much good at that."

I could read that she was thinking of her uncle taking in strays—her and Adam.

"Why are you here ... I mean, why have you moved here?" Adam asked.

Ophelia looked surprised. "Didn't Uncle Seb tell you?"

"No, he just said his niece was coming to live with him and we decided we'd make the bachelor pad downstairs and you could take the upstairs."

"My parents died."

"Shit."

"Yeah, kills a conversation," she shrugged. "So Uncle Seb is my closest living relative. He's mum's brother. Dad's got a few sisters but one is overseas and the other, well I don't really know her and she didn't want kids."

Adam nodded. "You could do worse. He's a really nice guy your uncle." They had reached the Surf Life Savers Club and he turned to walk back. So did I as I stayed with them.

They stopped momentarily to watch several board riders taking on a sizeable wave. Two were smashed, rolling head-over-heels as their boards surfaced before them; one surfer rode the wave in. He jumped off in the shallow water and grabbed his board. Seeing he had an audience, he smiled at Ophelia and gave Adam a begrudging nod. No love lost between those two, never has been.

"Know him?" Ophelia asked watching the tall, blond surfer head back out into the ocean.

"Yep. Ready to walk back?" Adam said.

Ophelia grinned.

"What? Adam asked, smiling at her.

"Clearly you don't like him."

He shrugged. "Chayse Johann—he's alright, a bit full of himself.

He lives in Warrnambool and usually surfs there, don't know why he's down here."

"Better waves?" she suggested.

Adam shrugged. "There's a bit of family history stuff with him ... more a grudge on his side than ours."

Ophelia looked out to sea; the hairs on her arm stood on end. Not far from the beach the water became a dark blue, menacing and deep. I loved it like that. She would too one day, hopefully.

"It's amazing to think there are ships still lying out there," she shuddered.

"Even freakier to dive around them, or so I've heard," he laughed but it sounded hollow.

They walked on until the track to the house came into sight and Ophelia called the dogs closer. They could see Sebastian looking out to sea at the attic window, watching the sunset on the horizon.

"I could pull anything over Uncle Seb, he is not sure what I'm supposed to do at my age. He even offered me his car keys," she said.

Adam laughed. "So you have to apply your own curfew and send yourself to your room?"

"Apparently."

"Could be fun," he flashed her a smile.

Ophelia blushed and they finished the walk in silence.

Don't fall for him Ophelia I whispered as I walked beside them.

CHAPTER 5

OPHELIA

I couldn't sleep; back to my old routine. I rarely slept right through the night since Mum and Dad ... you know. I miss them so much my chest aches sometimes and then I won't think about them for a few hours and then I feel terrible that I've forgotten them. I have a photo of each of them in a locket—I know it is old-fashioned but I can keep them close, against my skin.

It's funny this new life; Uncle Seb is so lovely and seems really okay with me being here. School was better than I thought and Adam ... it's kind of good to have a big brother, someone who has my back. I'm glad he's not at school; it is good to have friends from different worlds. I still feel like I'm in a spotlight at school, I guess that will stop when everyone is used to me.

I heard the clock in the hallway strike three. The room was so lit; moonlight streamed in around the curtain edges and filtered through the netting around my bed. The moon must have been hanging right outside my window. I rose and went to the window, pushing back the curtains. It was a full moon and I was right, it was spectacular and just tipping the edge of the ocean. It was so bright it might as well have been a street light.

I sat on the wide timber window seat in the bay window and pulled my legs up, hooking my arms around my knees. I looked out to sea—it was both beautiful and scary. The dark ocean, the waves crashing close to shore and the ghostly glow of the moon and then, I saw him. I thought I had imagined it the first day but no, it was the same figure I saw for just those few moments.

I jumped up and reached for the curtain pulling it almost shut again, but he wasn't looking up at me, he hadn't noticed the curtains open—he was looking amongst the rocks. I studied him through the gap in the curtain; he looked about the same age as me, maybe a few years older. His hair was light—tasselled and wind-swept, short at the sides—he wore dark pants, black boots and a big navy knitted jumper. What was he doing down there on the rocks at three ... I looked at the clock beside the bed ... three-fifteen in the morning? I watched him sit on the largest rock and stare across the ocean. Must be so cold out there.

If Mum and Dad were still here, I would never have considered going down to the beach to meet him—I guess if Mum and Dad were around I wouldn't be here anyway. But maybe feeling numb over the last few months increased my sense of risk, after all, what's the worst that could happen? Death. Yeah, I've met that and it doesn't scare me much anymore.

I was still contemplating going down to meet him when he looked straight up at the window at me. I jumped back—it gave me a hell of a fright. Well, might as well go down now that he's seen me spying. I tentatively peeped out from between the curtains again and he was gone! I glanced around the beach and the rock area, and up the path to the house but he was gone, disappeared like a ghost.

I must have gone back to sleep after watching the guy on the beach because I woke up at seven o'clock. I went to the bathroom, showered, dressed and headed down to grab some toast. I dropped my school bag near the front door. Uncle Seb was up and sitting at a bench beside the kitchen window where he could see the ocean. His hair was still slightly damp from the shower and he was dressed in jeans, and a long sleeve shirt—his usual workwear. He had an empty bowl in front of him and the cereal packet was still on the kitchen bench counter. Agnes and Argo trotted over to greet me and I kissed them both on the head. Adam was nowhere in sight, probably already gone to work.

"Sleep well?" Uncle Seb asked.

"Nope. And you?"

"I usually do," he answered. "A combination of too much thinking during the day and the smell of salt air at night … delightful. Want me to cook you some eggs?"

"No, but thanks. I'm good with toast. Want some?"

He shook his head. "Are you worried?" Uncle Seb asked.

"About what?"

"Anything? Is that why you are not sleeping?" he rose and going to the kettle flicked it on. He reached for a second cup for me and threw a teabag in his and mine.

I shrugged. "No, I just don't sleep a lot."

"But you used to?" Uncle Seb persisted.

"I guess so."

He nodded and poured boiling water into our cups. I reached past him and pushed a piece of bread down into the toaster.

"I'm sorry Lia. I wish I could help more."

"You don't have to Uncle Seb, you've done plenty. I love being here."

"Do you?" he grinned. "That's a relief."

I smiled and looked away. I was a bit blown away that he seemed genuinely happy to have me here.

"I thought I might have cramped your style," I said accepting the tea from him after he added the milk.

Uncle Seb scoffed. "I think you can see I have no style. Argo and

Agnes are my kids and we just hang here with the house don't we kids?"

Argo barked on cue again on hearing his name, and Agnes appeared to nod.

"Now," Uncle Seb continued, "we're a family of five, hanging with the house." He returned to his bench seat near the window and I spread some butter and Vegemite on my toast.

"You know there are counsellors and doctors who deal with grief if you wanted to chat to someone who knew what they were doing," Uncle Seb offered. "It would be no trouble to organise it."

"I've had some counselling," I told him. "They gave it to me before I came here. Have you ever had counselling before?" I sat down on a stool near him with my breakfast.

Uncle Seb nodded. "I was married once."

"Really? I didn't know that," I said.

"I was only about twenty-two. But my wife, Meg, she died and I had a bit of counselling."

The house howled and the windows upstairs shook.

Uncle Seb looked up the staircase. "Thank you," he said to the house. Yep, positively weird.

"How did she die? If it's okay to ask?" I sipped on my tea.

"She drowned," Uncle Seb swallowed and glanced out the window. "Out there," he said.

I gasped without thinking, his answer was a shock.

"Very early one morning," Uncle Seb explained. "I don't know why she was on the rocks or what happened but someone saw her fall in and when they raced to help her, they couldn't find her. It was still dark, just before dawn," he shrugged.

"That's awful," I said looking out to the treacherous rock. "Did you find Meg, eventually?"

"Oh yes, later that day she washed ashore. So very strange, she was a capable swimmer."

"She must have slipped, perhaps hit her head ..." I struggled to say something right. I knew from personal experience it was hard to say the right thing. "How long were you together?"

"We started dating in the last year of high school, got married after Uni and she died two years after that," Uncle Seb said. He delivered the words without emotion as if he had said this a thousand times.

"That's terrible," I said, "terrible." There was not one photo of Meg or the two of them in the house.

"A long time ago now," Uncle Seb said, as he rose. "But I understand why you are not sleeping, Lia. But you will again, I promise."

We heard a commotion at the door and Argo and Agnes jumped up and began to bark. Their tales wagged furiously as Harry and Holly appeared in the window. Holly waved and Uncle Seb let them in.

"Hey, thought we'd all walk to the bus station together," Harry said.

"Great idea," Uncle Seb said. "Leave those dishes, Lia," he directed me as I started to the sink. "I've got plenty of time."

Holly was playing tug-of-war with Argo.

"It was my idea," she said. "We walk by every day this time if you want to meet us at the gate."

"It would have been my idea if you hadn't beaten me to it," Harry interrupted his twin sister.

I grinned and looked to Uncle Seb who was shaking his head at the two of them.

"See what I have to put up with every day," Holly rolled her eyes. "Where's Adam?"

"He's left for work," Uncle Seb said.

"Got your lunch?" Harry asked me, as I picked up my school bag near the door.

"Ah, lunch! I didn't think of it. I haven't prepared anything for you yet, Lia." He started for the kitchen.

"It's okay Uncle Seb, really. I haven't had a packed lunch since primary school, but thanks," I assured him.

"I'll have a packed lunch if you don't want it," Harry piped up.

"Money then, you'll need to buy lunch," he headed towards his office.

"I'm good, really, I've got cash," I called after him stopping him in his tracks. "Bye Argo, bye Agnes, see you Uncle Seb." I pushed Harry out the door in front of me and stopped to let Holly go next.

"Yeah, bye Uncle Seb," Harry called.

I heard Uncle Seb laugh. I bet he wonders what he got himself into. At the bottom of the driveway, I looked back and saw him watching through the windows, a dog on each side and the house looking surprised—I gave him a wave.

~

HOLLY

She looked tired, the new girl—funny how the new person is always the new person until someone else comes along. Anyway, her eyes were dark. I put a black makeup pencil around mine to get the dark look but she was so pale, that her eyes just stood out. We sat next to each other on the bus and Harry dropped into the seat in front of us, extended over it and turned side-on so he didn't miss the conversation. I could tell he liked her already; I couldn't read Ophelia but I don't think Harry was in her zone. I decided to find out who was in her zone.

"So did you talk with Adam?" I asked her.

"Pretty hard not to when he lives there with her," Harry piped up.

Ophelia nodded and said in a low voice. "We took the dogs for a walk along the beach last night."

44

"Really? I'm so jealous." I think I squealed then lowered my voice. "I've had a crush on Adam Ferrier since ... well forever! He's gorgeous—those dreamy, deep blue eyes and cute smile," I daydreamed for a moment then remembered I wasn't alone. "Half the girls in school have a crush on him or did when he was at school anyway. He was seeing Vanessa Jones in the year above us, but they split."

"What do the chicks see in him? I mean what's he got that I haven't?" Harry interrupted us. I looked at my twin brother with his ginger hair and freckles, his green eyes and slightly out of proportion nose. Whatever, someone would fall in love with him eventually. I ignored him and turned my attention back to Ophelia. "Do you like him?"

"Sure," Ophelia answered. "He said to think of him as my big brother and that he would have my back. I like that."

"I'd rather think of him as a boyfriend," I said. "If you want my advice, don't let him see you first thing in the morning yet ... you don't want to scare him off too early."

"But we're all living together ... kind of like Uncle Seb's extended family of strays," she smiled.

"And I'm sure Lia's head is better than yours in the morning," my brother added. I continued to ignore him.

"I wish I could be that close to him," I sighed again. "I even love the name Adam. Adam ... Adam and Holly, Adam and Holly Ferrier."

"Give it up," Harry said bringing me back to earth.

Ophelia started laughing and I joined in.

"Just make sure you don't keep him out near midnight," Harry muttered.

I nudge Harry and give him a warning look. I don't think Ophelia saw it.

∼

OPHELIA

Harry, Holly and I were in the same class for nearly every subject except I did accounting while they took biology and we were all in different sport houses. I felt a bit sorry for Holly—her two best friends left at the end of year ten; one took up an apprentice chef role and the other went to Sydney with her parents when her father changed jobs. She still saw Sally, the apprentice on weekends, but she was almost as lost as I was—good for both of us that we bonded.

I came from biology class and when I entered the history classroom Holly and Harry hadn't arrived. I drew a deep breath and continued walking in; I dreaded entering a room and having to find a seat and try not to take someone else's seat or look pathetic and sit on my own.

I was relieved to see Peggy sitting in the corner and she waved me over and pointed at the seat next to her.

"I know what you're thinking," Peggy started talking before I could say hello. I smiled a greeting and dropped down beside her.

"What am I thinking?" I asked. I was pretty sure Peggy wouldn't guess I was thinking about Adam and that guy I saw on the rocks at three o'clock this morning. Who was he?

Peggy drew a deep breath and said with confidence, "you're thinking what project topic should you pick this term? Me too, but I think I've worked it out."

"Of course. I was definitely going to be thinking about that soon," I agreed, any day now for sure. Peggy was about to continue when a well-rounded, stocky man entered the room. Half a dozen students including Harry and Holly raced in behind him before he closed the door. Holly waved in my direction and dropped into a seat near the door.

"Just made it," the teacher threatened them.

"That's Mr Meadows, we had him for history last year too," Peggy whispered.

"A bit of quiet," he called. "Project selection time for the term!"

The class groaned.

"Yes, I knew you would be excited too." He glanced around the room. "Good to see a new face. Welcome, Miss?"

"Ophelia ... Ophelia Montague," I said, again.

"Ah, now there's a name from history, literary history at least ... from Shakespeare's Hamlet. But you all knew that of course," he smiled indulgently.

Peggy nodded. The rest of the class looked blank.

Mr Meadows continued. "So those of you who were in my class last term, which is all of you except Ophelia, will know we have one exam, one individual project and one team project for your assessment. This term, you will be doing your individual projects. You have one week to give me your topic for approval."

The class groaned again.

"Does anyone besides Peggy know what they are doing?" Mr Meadows asked. Peggy looked surprised. "I'm just guessing you've got that sorted?" he said to her.

She nodded. "I was thinking about what form World War III might take if there was going to be one and how different it would be from World War I and II—you know, better weapons, who might be enemies and allies. Is that okay?" Peggy asked, looking worried. I'm sure she's probably top of the class but always a worrier.

"More than okay, that's great. But if you find it gets too big, just select one of the wars to compare it to ... maybe the last one, World War II since it was more sophisticated in weaponry and warfare, supposedly," Mr Meadows said.

A few hands shot up.

"Russell McCannes, is that your hand I see up before me? Let me sit down before the shock kills me," Mr Meadows moved towards a chair.

The class laughed and Russell grinned. "I'm going to discuss if the United Nations has a role as a peacekeeper ... or if they are just a waste of space."

Mr Meadows nodded. "So eloquently phrased. That sounds good Russell, very good, permission granted." He looked at the few other hands remaining up and pointed to an attractive Indian girl in the front row. "Nami, what's your proposed topic?"

"I was going to do the rise of India and China as possible superpowers, Sir," she said.

"Love it Nami, go right ahead."

He turned his gaze to me. "So Ophelia, that's the sort of project topics we need. Everyone has until this Friday to pitch their idea."

"I have an idea, Sir," I said. What the heck, might as well get it over with.

"Good, shoot ..."

"Just to familiarise myself with the area, I was going to do the history of shipwreck's on this West Coast and look at how much was human error. It's probably been done a lot before though I guess," I shrugged.

"There's plenty of material around but I think looking at what was human error, what was an act of God—like the weather—and what was structural like the fault of the ships and materials, would be an interesting comparison. Well done," he said impressed. "There's a couple of students you should speak with who are descended from shipwreck families. Anyone in this class?"

Garth Dart raised his hand. "We're descendant from the *Julia*, Sir. William Dart was the captain and my great, great, something."

The class laughed again. At least Mr Meadows' classes were going to be lively.

"What's the *Julia* story then Garth?" Mr Meadows continued.

"She lost her rudder in heavy seas, Sir, and came a cropper against the rocks. A whaleboat with six men on board came out to help and all the crew from the *Julia* survived, but six of the whalers died helping to rescue them."

Several female students gasped.

"Well thanks for that cheery tale, Garth," Mr Meadows said. "There you go Ophelia, have a chat to Garth. Also, in the year above you is Chayse Johann. He lost distant relatives on the La Bella."

"And he's gorgeous," one of the girls in front of me giggled.

"And he's gorgeous, thank you, Jane, that will be of great assistance to Ophelia with her project," Mr Meadows teased and Jane went bright red. "Right," he continued, "let's begin with today's subject—the world at the beginning of the 20th century."

The class groaned again.

After class, Peggy invited me to join her for lunch and we headed out into the common area. We sat under a huge tree in the shade.

"That's Chayse Johann over there," Peggy nodded towards a tall, handsome blond student surrounded by a group of good looking other students, and one girl in particular hanging of him. He had hair to his shoulders and was tanned and athletic.

Harry and Holly dropped down on the grass beside us.

"Who are we looking at?" Holly asked.

"Chayse Johann," Peggy said. "You know, Mr Meadows said Ophelia should chat to him for her shipwreck project."

"I'd talk to him if I could," Holly said, "but I can't speak in his presence. I get tongue-tied."

"So he's tall, sporty, blond and rich," Harry shrugged. "Big deal."

"Yeah big deal," Peggy said fluttering her eyelashes at Harry. Ah ha, Peggy likes Harry and Harry ... seems oblivious. I'll have to work on that—yeah, fast worker ... here for a few days, I've got the locals sorted, met a guy on the beach and am matchmaking Peggy and Harry. Makes you wonder how they got by before I came, I kidded myself and then felt a wave of missing my best friend.

I heard a shrill laugh rise from Chayse's group and we all looked over again. The girls in his pack were looking at him adoringly and one snuggled in closer to him—she was beautiful. I don't think I'll be asking Chayse Johann anything. I can't imagine getting through the pack to even get close enough to spring a question on him.

"I've seen him around," I said and pulled my skirt down as I stretched my legs out in front of me on the grass. "He was surfing yesterday afternoon and rode a wave all the way in. He said hi but gave Adam a bit of a shirty look."

"Yeah no love lost there," Harry said.

"Why?" I asked looking over at Chayse again.

"Long story," Harry started before Holly interrupted him with gossip.

"That beautiful girl hanging off Chayse is his girlfriend, Imogen Harper ... she's so full of herself. Why do beautiful girls always have to be full of themselves?" Holly sighed.

"Amber's not," Peggy said. "Neither is Alice."

"Yeah, that's true," Holly agreed.

"Neither are you three," Harry said.

We all looked at him and smiled. Smooth, Harry. I didn't know the girls they were talking about but I studied Imogen Harper, Chayse's girlfriend. She was beautiful—a beach type with blond hair, super slim with a glowing, natural tan but she was bigger up top already than most of my class and the seniors. She had a body that probably looked great in a bikini.

"She suits Chayse," I said, "they look good together, like Barbie and Ken." I glanced down at my own white 'city' arms. "I look more like a vampire than a surf girl."

"Vampires are in," Harry assured me. Two compliments, sort of. Harry was going to win on charm if nothing else.

"You and Imogen have something in common—your names are both from Shakespeare plays," Peggy said. "Dried apricot?" she offered the bag around and we all tried one.

"You'll have to get by Imogen and her flock to get to Chayse," Holly said, ignoring the literary connection. "She's always with him, very territorial."

"But she's gorgeous," I stated the obvious. "Surely she has guys after her too. She can't be that insecure that she has to hang off him."

Holly shrugged.

"Maybe he doesn't make her feel secure," Peggy offered with

great wisdom. We all turned to look at her and she blushed. "That's what happens in *Bold and Beautiful*. They get really clingy until they've won the guy over."

I sighed looking back at Chayse. "Yeah, well I can live without his shipwreck version of events." Just as I said that he looked right at me. For some reason only known to the universe, he must have recognised me from the beach yesterday and he raised his hand in a wave. *Way to go new girl ... great way to make new friends*. I felt everyone turn to look at me. I smiled and waved back and looked away super quickly.

"OMG!" Holly said, "Chayse just waved to you ... and you should see the death stare his girlfriend is giving you."

Peggy grinned. "You've got an admirer already, Lia!"

I shook my head. "No he just recognises me from the beach yesterday; I'm just that girl who was with Adam."

"It's good to have an admirer though," Peggy said, pulling at her long dark plait and with a glance in Harry's direction, again. "You know the first dance is only two months away."

Harry groaned. "That means I've got to start hiding now ... Paige Stark will be after me."

Peggy frowned. Harry couldn't see her.

CHAPTER 6

JACK

*O*phelia couldn't see me but as soon as she was opposite the beach, I had her in sight as she walked up the path to the front door of what was now her home. She smiled seeing Argo and Agnes lying in the warmth of the sun on either side of the door. She had a nice smile but her face was so pale that she looked positively translucent. Argo and Agnes spotted her and ran down the path to greet her with a raucous round of barking and energy. She seemed really delighted to see them and dropped her backpack to embrace them both.

"Is Uncle Seb home?" I heard her ask the dogs and looked to his office window to the right of the door. Hearing the noise, he appeared in the window and waved.

Ophelia picked up her bag and went to push open the door but it swung in easily. The dogs followed her in. I stayed outside, hearing but not seeing. The house moaned, it could sense me nearby.

"Hi Lia," I heard Sebastian call from the hallway. "I've got a conference call in five minutes so I'll be out in about half an hour."

"All good," she called back and I heard her thump up the stairs two at a time to her level and to her room. She called out: "Can I take Argo and Agnes for a walk up the beach?"

"Absolutely, thanks!" Sebastian called back.

Excellent. I withdrew down the driveway towards the beach waiting for her to appear. I had been waiting for her all day, unable to get her out of my mind since seeing her framed by moonlight in the window last night—she looked beautiful and ghostly.

Within minutes she reappeared wearing fitted grey three-quarter leggings, an oversized black hoodie, her hair tied back and peeking through a black baseball cap. At the front door, she pushed her feet into her white canvas slip-ons, grab the dogs' leads which were more for show-and-tell in case needed, and closing the door behind her, headed to the beach. The two dogs shook their tails with excitement and flanked her like guard dogs.

I walked in her shadow. I saw her stop as she got to the end of the path and the beach entrance, slip off the shoes, and enjoy the cool sand between her toes. She breathed in deeply; the air was full of salt, so thick you could almost cut it. The dogs obediently stopped and waited for her. They all headed to the firm sand. For big dogs, they moved well; Agnes and Argo chased each other, running to the water's edge. Ophelia glanced left and right and decided to walk the opposite way to her walk last evening with Adam. The dogs ran ahead.

I walked nearby her. I whispered her name into the wind. She turned sharply left and then right, but could not see me. Her hand reached for the locket around her throat and she touched it, believing the sound she heard was her parents. I could read her thoughts and her energy. She was pleased for the time alone; time to think about her parents. She smiled at the dogs enjoying themselves as they ran back to her side and back to the water's edge again. Out to sea she could see a ship on the horizon and knew Sebastian would be excited watching from his office window. Further down the beach a couple of joggers ran past us but otherwise, the beach was largely deserted. At the point, the surfers were out catching the remaining waves of the day.

This was nice, very nice; just the two of us and Agnes and Argo. I felt like I had her all to myself. She breathed deeply again and followed the dogs to the water's edge to walk in the firmer sand. I could do this every day, Ophelia. We could do it together. Like trained protectors, Agnes and Argo took turns at coming back and checking on her; neither going too far ahead. Maybe they sensed me, so did Ophelia; she shuddered walking through a cold pocket of air. She walked on for another fifteen minutes or so, the ocean breeze gently keeping her hair off her face and masking her with salt water spray. As she neared the point, she saw a group of six people on the beach watching the surfers. Ophelia shivered—it was chilly out there, they were diehards. She called the names of both the dogs and when they joined her, she told them it was time to turn, and they began to walk back the other way.

As I walked, behind her, we both heard her name being called. I knew who it was—like vultures these men looking at new prey. First Adam Ferrier, now Chayse Johann. He was heading out of the water, his surfboard tucked under his arm. He called out her name again.

"Ophelia, wait up."

She stopped and the dogs rejoined her. I waited nearby as Ophelia watched him head up the beach and pull the surfboard strap from his leg. He dropped his board on the sand, grabbed his towel and ran towards her. I felt Ophelia's heart racing—he was tall, handsome and glowing, his tanned skin wet and his hair slicked back. She could see why he was the school heartthrob but not her type, I was sure of that.

"Hey," he caught up to her. "We haven't officially met, I'm Chayse."

"Hi, I'm Ophelia," she offered her hand.

His large tanned hand enveloped it.

"I know. We don't get many newcomers at school in year eleven or twelve, especially mid-year. When did you arrive?" he asked. He ran his hand through his hair and shook out the excess water.

"Last week. You're good," she said with a nod to the waves.

"Yeah well I'd want to be. I've been surfing since I could walk."

Ophelia smiled at him not sure what to say.

"You're living with Sebastian," he said more as a statement than a question.

"Yes, he's my uncle. He's been good enough to take me in."

"Yeah, I heard about … well, I'm sorry," Chayse said. He looked at her sincerely and held her gaze.

Ophelia nodded. "Thank you." She looked back out to sea. Clearing her throat she asked, "Can I ask a favour?" Argo came and stood beside her and Ophelia ran her hand over Argo's silky head.

"So soon?" he grinned.

Ophelia reddened. "It's no big deal if you don't want to."

"Ask away."

"I'm doing a history paper on the shipwreck history of the area, cause and effect—Mr Meadows said you're a descendent with a shipwreck past and might tell me your story," Ophelia shrugged. "But only if you have time and want to … it's no big …"

He cut her off. "Love to. Maybe this weekend we could catch up, if you're free?"

Ophelia nodded. "That would be great. I don't know too many people here yet so I'm free all the time at the moment."

Chayse laughed. "Well good of you to fit me in then."

My heart leaped. I wanted Ophelia to myself this weekend. I willed him to leave.

"I think you're wanted," Ophelia said. I saw her glance behind Chayse to see his stunning blond girlfriend looking gorgeous in a very small white bikini bottom and cropped top. Clearly she was oblivious to the cold as she stood near his towel looking at them from a distance, her hands on her hips. She was more his type than Ophelia, I hope he remembered that.

Ophelia raised her hand and gave Imogen a wave, which was reluctantly returned. Good move though.

Chayse glanced behind and then back to Ophelia. He looked annoyed, running his hand over his face and through his hair.

"I've got to get home, thanks for agreeing to be my research subject," she smiled and turned, leading Argo and Agnes away.

"Anytime," he called behind her. "See you tomorrow at school, we can swap numbers then."

Ophelia glanced back, nodded and smiled. She walked on beside me, feeling me and touching her locket again. The dogs raced ahead. After a moment or so, she glanced back to see Chayse's girlfriend draping herself over him reclaiming her territory. It was time that I staked mine.

CHAPTER 7

OPHELIA

I saw him again that night, well early morning. It was like he controlled the moon and shone it into my bedroom. It leaked through the curtains, hanging suspended out the front of our home in the middle of the ocean. It was just after three o'clock when I stirred and decided to rise. Sometimes, when I can't sleep, the only answer is to get up and do something. I had to keep the noise down however so I didn't wake Uncle Seb, Adam and the furry kids.

I decided to sit in the bay window in my room again and watch the ocean, maybe I would see a ship on the horizon or some of the trawlers coming in. I pulled track pants and a knit pullover on over my T-shirt and underpants and prying open some of the curtain, slipped into the bay window seat. I turned to look down below and jumped in fright. He was there again, the same guy, this time he stood on the rocks looking directly up at me, his hands in his coat pockets, as though he had been waiting for me to appear.

My heart was beating so fast from the fright. I could easily make out his smile like he was enjoying the joke. He looked down at the rocks a bit sheepishly then back up at me again. He had on a long jacket, like a military jacket that went to his knees, with dark pants and black boots. He looked strikingly handsome. His smile was infectious, a bit cheeky, and then he raised his hand and beckoned me down.

I felt a shiver of fear and excitement. I bit my lip while I thought about it—he could be an axe murderer or he could attack me and then next day everyone would say how stupid I was to be down there on the rocks at that hour. He cocked his head to the side like he was trying to read my thoughts, then he looked down at the rocks again, nudged something with his boot, and pushing his hands into his coat pocked, he turned back around to look out to sea.

I jumped up; I was going to go meet him. I put my runners on and grabbed from the cupboard a long, black waterproof jacket that Uncle Seb had given me on my arrival. I tied it up and carefully opened my door. There was not a sound. I crept down the stairs and met Argo at the bottom of the staircase. I patted him and he returned to his bed. I tugged the door open, snuck out and moved quickly across the path to the beach's edge. I expected him to be gone again as I walked out on the sand and turned right towards the rock and rock pools. But there he was, striding from rock to rock, bending down and wading his hand through the rock pools. He caught sight of me and stood to full height.

I shivered with the cold or maybe expectation. I must be crazy going out to meet a guy on the beach at three a.m. Who does that except in those horror movies that you watch through your fingers and scream out "turn the light on" or "don't go in there, go back, go back!" I was getting carried away. He looked as nervous as I was, and smiled a beautiful smile. He was about a head taller than me and pale too. I could see a scar near his eyebrow and the top of a tattoo on his neck, the rest of the tattoo disappearing beneath his jacket line.

"Hello moonlight girl," he said in a warm tone.

I smiled. "Ophelia," I told him.

He repeated my name.

"And you are?" I asked.

"Pleased to meet you at last," he said. "I thought you would never come. I'm Jack." He held out his hand. "Jack Denham."

I took his hand and I can't explain what happened. It was some kind of connection. It sounds crazy to say but it was as if I had always known him, like I needed to know him. Then he let my hand go.

JACK

She was so beautiful. I knew the moment I set eyes on her that I would have her, but when we touched I was a little overwhelmed by the electricity—I had to let her hand go. I'm sure we were destined; some people don't believe that but I have always believed that souls are made in pairs. Everyone else that you meet is just a learning experience, but one person is made just for you and you don't want to lose that chance to be with them.

"Why are you up at this hour?" she asked me. "I've seen you before haven't I?

"You did see me then?" I answered.

She nodded. "I thought I was seeing a ghost."

"Is that a bad thing?" I teased her.

She smiled again, bit her lower lip and looked out to sea.

I watched her, not wanting to take my eyes from her face. "I could ask the same thing of you ... what are you doing up at this hour?"

"I guess we're both restless souls," she shrugged.

"I feel calm now," I told her.

Her eyes searched my face, she wasn't sure about me or why she felt the chemistry but I knew she did as well.

I offered my hand to her. "Come and sit on the rock with me for a while and watch the moon and tides for a bit? We don't have to talk if you don't want to."

She looked surprised like I had read her thoughts, which I had.

"That would be good," she sighed ever so softly. "When you're new, everyone wants to talk and hear your story."

"And telling it is like opening a wound," I said.

"Do you know ... about me?" her brow furrowed as she looked at me.

"No," I answered, "but I know about me."

"Oh," she said, realising that I might not want to share my story just yet. She stepped towards me and placed her hand in mine. I led her up the rocks and guided her as she jumped over some of the little rock pools.

"You have a slight accent," she narrowed her eyes studying me. "Or you speak ... well, formally."

"I didn't notice," I shrugged.

"It's nice," she assured me. "Are you a local?"

"I am," I told her. I had been here for a very, very long time already.

She fell into me once and I reluctantly straightened her.

"Sorry," she blushed.

"I'm not," I said making her blush even more. I picked a spot that I knew would remain high and dry and where the moon would look magical and we sat until dawn.

When she had to leave, I helped her back to the sand. I watched her leave before Adam and her uncle were up and the house stirred into action. I was gone before she looked out of her bedroom window for me, but I knew she would look. Our bond was meant to be and I missed her already.

CHAPTER 8

OPHELIA

"You haven't stopped yawning all morning," Peggy prodded me at lunchtime. "Did you stay up late studying?"

Harry scoffed. "It's the second week of term!"

"Just because you don't study, doesn't mean other people aren't cramming," Holly told her twin.

I saw Peggy nod. She was hesitant to go against Harry but she agreed with Holly. I noticed she was trying a few different hairstyles now that she had closer access to Harry through me. I think Harry remained clueless to her charms.

"There was a fight last night," Harry said, saving me from having to explain my nocturnal happenings to Peggy.

"Yeah and Adam came off worse," Holly added. She took the band from her wrist and tied her bleached blond hair back as a light wind whipped between us.

My ears pricked up at the mention of Adam's name. "What happened? Was Adam hurt? But he was home last night."

Harry took over the telling of the story. "Must have gone out for a while around nine, it was down in front of the surf club—Adam and

Chayse at it again but Adam took the punishment. He's alright; he walked home."

"I didn't see him this morning ... but he did turn in early last night. He must have gone back out." I tried to remember. "What were they fighting about?" I scanned the grounds for Chayse and his pack but couldn't see them.

Harry looked at Holly and back at me and shrugged. "I don't know really, some family grudge that goes back a long time."

I frowned. "But ... I don't get it."

Holly stepped in. "It's complex."

Peggy rolled her eyes. "Adam's great, great, well ancestor, named William Ferrier, saved some of the sailors on the La Bella, but he couldn't save one of Chayse's relatives. He and the other rescuers could only reach so many because of the size of the sea. "

"Well that's hardly Adam's fault and I'm sure William saved as many as he could," I said. "Really, they're fighting about that?"

"No," Peggy continued. "The widow of Chayse's ancestor moved here so she could be close to where her husband drew his last breath —romantic huh?" she said with a glance to Harry and then continued. "She already had three sons, so the Johann name continued on in this town. But the Johann clan was always angry because the town celebrated Adam's ancestor and other heroes in the town with statues and the annual Seafarer's Parade, but never acknowledged those who lost their lives here. They thought they should be remembered too."

"Ah," it started to dawn on me. "So they begrudged the Ferriers for their status in the community and since then there has been this rivalry over the generations, sort of?"

"Precisely," Holly piped in. "Especially when you're talking men," she said rolling her eyes and glancing at Harry.

"What?" he held up his hands. "I wouldn't be that stupid."

We all considered that for a moment and moved on.

Holly said, "So for generations they've hated each other and taunted each other, and even if you got Chayse and Adam together to talk about why they hated each other I bet they couldn't really tell you. But it's in their blood."

"That's dopey," I added.

Peggy laughed.

"And Chayse is taller and bigger than Adam, he should lay off," I added.

Harry scoffed again. "Don't worry, Adam held his own. He's fit, fast and good with his fists."

Holly, Peggy and I grimaced.

"And you know about the midnight curse?" Peggy said.

I saw Holly and Harry exchange looks.

"No," I looked at them suspiciously and then back to Peggy. I remember now that Harry said something about Adam not staying out after midnight. I caught it in my peripheral hearing first or second day on the bus, but there was so much else going on I forgot it.

"It's nothing, just a joke," Holly said. "A sort of myth or legend, that's all."

"No, it's not," Peggy said full of knowledge. "It's a curse." She turned back to me relishing her role as storyteller. "Because the widow was said to have heard her husband call her name right as the clock struck midnight—when he died, despite the fact he was here and she was on the other side of the earth—it is said that she wept so many tears that all surviving sailors and their descendants if they were near the ocean at midnight, would be swept out to sea in her ocean of tears and drown like her husband."

I smirked at them. "Yeah right. Have they tested this mythical legend?"

"Yeah," Peggy said, wide-eyed. "Two of Adam's descendants have drowned at sea after midnight."

"Really?" I frowned trying to read from their faces if they were having me on. "This is too weird. You're freaking me out."

"It's just a myth," Harry shrugged, "an old wives' tale as Mum calls it."

"But it scares Adam enough that he won't test it?" I asked.

No-one answered.

"I wonder if that's why his parents move all the time? Not tempting fate maybe," Peggy said.

"What if he's out after midnight and goes nowhere near the ocean?" I asked.

Holly looked around. "Nearly everywhere around here is near the ocean. If you want my advice, just don't agree to any midnight beach walks with him!"

I couldn't concentrate all afternoon in class, I had to see Adam. I hoped he was okay. Luckily Peggy and I had history for the last two classes and we could use the time for our projects since my concentration was shot. I hit the library to begin my shipwreck research for the history project. I went online, gathered all I could on the shipwreck history of the area, the shipwreck trail and some reference points where I could look at original news clippings.

I felt his presence before I saw him; Chayse Johann dropped down into the seat next to me. He glowed with strength like he stored the sun when surfing.

"Ophelia," he smiled.

"Hi Chayse," I looked around, he was alone. "No harem?"

He grinned and had the good grace to look a bit embarrassed. "They're my friends actually."

"Oh, sorry, my mistake," I teased him. I studied his face. Adam did land a few blows—Chayse was bruised above his eye and his nose was swollen slightly. There was a cut on his left cheek.

"What happened to you?" I asked, knowing full well.

He reached up and touched the bruise above his eye. "Ah, nothing, just a friendly fight."

I nodded. "Does it hurt?"

He shrugged. "A little. But he's hurting more," he smiled.

"Poor guy."

Chayse realised he was losing out on the sympathy.

"Oh don't worry, he held his own. Got me a good one in the ribs," he rubbed them. "Couldn't breathe for a moment there."

I sat back and turned slightly to face him. He was gorgeous, I could see why Holly got tongue-tied around him. I bet he'd had a charmed life so far.

"Can you tell me your shipwreck story, if you have time now?" I asked.

"Now? Sure," he leaned back and flashed a smile at me. "Once upon a time on a dark and stormy night ..."

I laughed. "Can I have the real version, not the fairytale?"

"Oh, right, the real version, okay," he pulled his chair closer to mine. I hoped his girlfriend didn't come by now, I would be on the deathwatch list. I leaned back away from him and he got the hint and backed off a bit.

"The year was 1905 and my great, great, great grandfather, Pierre, that's three greats right?" he asked.

"Three greats, I'm paying attention," I said. "Pierre, huh?"

"Yes, Pierre," he said with a French accent and rewarded me with his smile again and carried on. "He was on a ship called La Bella. It had been in New Zealand where it was loaded up with timber. It was coming into Warrnambool which is dangerous at the best of times, but in 1905 with less technology to guide you, it was notorious. The seas were really heavy and there was the usual mist, you've seen it?"

"Thick as soup sometimes," I agreed.

"Imagine sailing blind in that?" Chayse shook his head. He was more interesting when he got over himself and was just real. "The captain got confused and the La Bella ran aground. It's called La Bella Reef now, the area where it ran aground. I'll show you sometime if you like."

"Sure," I said, keeping it short. I didn't want to interrupt the story.

"Anyway, the Warrnambool Harbour Master, his name was Captain Roe, seeing the La Bella was in distress, grabbed four lifesavers and they rowed out to help but they couldn't get near her because the waves were too huge. The La Bella crew lashed themselves to the port rails waiting for the lifeboat and hoping they wouldn't get washed out to sea."

Goosebumps raced up my arms. Chayse noticed and rubbed his hand over my arm, which just gave me more goosebumps.

"Must have been so frightening," I stuttered, trying to concentrate on his words and not his actions.

"Especially knowing you couldn't swim, not many of them could in those days," he said. "It was pretty wild out there and my ancestor Pierre, and two of the other men were the first to go. They were washed overboard around midnight. Another two died from exposure not long after but they were strapped to the ship, so the ropes kept them in place until about two in the morning when they were washed away. When the lifeboat finally reached the La Bella they rescued three of the crew. A local fisherman rowed his dinghy out and saved a few others. Another of the two sailors drowned trying to get to the lifeboat. Seven died, five survived."

I nodded. I had read a bit already and knew the basics of the story. Chayse didn't mention that the fisherman was Adam Ferrier's ancestor and couldn't swim or that he was incredibly brave to even go out in that wild ocean and risk being capsized himself.

Chayse drew a deep breath. "Finally, the La Bella was hit by a huge wave and the ship crashed down on the reef and broke up. The captain was later found guilty of careless navigation and he was suspended for twelve months. Got off lightly I'd say."

"Wow," I realised I had been holding my breath. "Is it weird to live near where the ship sunk, where Pierre drowned?"

"It's not weird ... but it's kind of ..." he searched for words, "it's sobering I guess. They say Pierre's wife used to walk the beach until the end of her days. She'd talk aloud as though he was walking beside her. But I think it is sad that the town doesn't acknowledge everyone who lost their lives at sea here. They're going to be here forever more if you know what I mean?" He ran a hand over his mouth as though he was worried what he said was too poetic for his image.

My heart swelled for Chayse; it was nice to see a side of him that wasn't all about being flashy.

He coughed and lowered his voice. "Sorry I get a bit carried away by this."

"It's in your blood," I said.

"Our blood has been boiling for generations," he almost hissed the words.

"So do something about it," I suggested. "Or am I overstepping the mark there?" I bit my lip waiting for an angry reaction. Instead, his eyes narrowed as he looked at me.

He nodded and rose. "Gotta' go, Ophelia, catch you around."

"Thanks for sharing the ..." he was gone, "... story."

CHAPTER 9

ADAM

I knew it wasn't going to be easy to avoid Ophelia but I didn't want her to see me looking black and blue. I managed to leave before she was up in the morning, but when I got to the beach that afternoon for a surf, she was walking around the rock pools with Argo and Agnes. I was going to try and sneak off in the opposite direction, but Chayse and his mates were surfing up that end of the beach and neither of us needed another encounter just yet. I wished he'd surf in his own turf.

Ophelia spotted me, and Argo and Agnes came bounding over. She looked so fragile—her hair was out, her jeans rolled up and she dug her hands into a large knitted jumper. Her eyes looked even lighter blue against the red of her jumper. I turned and waited for her.

"Hey," I said, looking at her briefly then out to the ocean. She didn't speak so I looked back at her and she was biting her lower lip.

"That looks bad," she said.

I shrugged and reached down to welcome Argo and Agnes.

"Chayse, huh?" she said.

"You heard?" I asked, "it was nothing."

She came closer; she smelt like powder, soft and sweet. She reached up to touch the cut and bruise above my right eye and I flinched—it was still throbbing with pain. I felt the warmth from the three fingers she placed on my skin.

"You might need a few stitches," she frowned, "that's a decent cut."

"No, it's fine thanks little sis," I shrugged her off with a grin.

"I am the woman of the house now, well Agnes and I are," she teased, "and we're to be obeyed in matters of first aid, women's business and well, Mrs Ducks can keep the cooking," she said. "No one should be inflicted with my beef stew."

"Feel free to practice your baking anytime you like," I encouraged her. "I miss Mum's cakes." I felt hungry thinking about them.

"Adam," she searched my face again, "I can't believe he did that to you."

My eye was black, I had cuts and scrapes on my left cheek and chin, and a deep cut above my right eye. Chayse had got a few blows in before I even got started.

"It's nothing, really," I assured her and stepped back. "He didn't get away lightly either, but I'm sure he told you that," I didn't mean to sound annoyed but I can imagine Chayse chatting her up at school and making himself out to be the victim to get her sympathy.

She smirked. "Where are you going in to surf? I'll walk that way."

"Okay," I picked up my board and started down the beach in the direction I wanted to have a paddle with Lia by my side. The dogs ran around us.

"You're both idiots," she said.

I laughed and dug the hand that wasn't holding the board into the warmth of my jumper pocket. "Yeah, well good thing I wasn't hanging out for any sympathy. Ever thought about being a nurse when you finish school? You'd be good at it," I teased her.

Ophelia flashed me a smile. "I'm not big on sympathy."

"I noticed—you don't give it and don't take it well." I remember how she brushed off my condolences when I tried to offer it. Still, I shouldn't have said that, she shut down. I cleared my throat and tried again. "It was his fault."

"Yeah, I'm sure he started it," she said.

I nodded. "He did."

"Or was it started like a century ago?" she asked. She pretended to chase Argo as he ran up to her.

"Well you know all about it," I said. "No need for me to fill you in." I did it again—I didn't mean to shut her down when she seemed genuinely concerned.

"You're very touchy about it," she said.

She was so direct I wasn't used to it. "Sorry," I muttered because I didn't know what to say.

We walked for a while enjoying the embracing cold air, talking about the beauty of the beach and her first few days at the new school. I knew people in her class; I was glad she was hanging with Holly and Peggy, they were nice. Harry was okay too.

"I'm writing a paper for school, for history," she said. "It would be really good if you would tell me the story of the La Bella from your family's perspective. Will you?" she asked, stopping beside me as I put the board down and stripped off my jumper. She clapped to get the dogs' attention.

I whistled for them and they came racing back at us, well as fast as two Great Danes could move with their big awkward limbs.

"I'd be happy to. One night over dinner maybe ... I mean dinner at home."

"Yeah I get it," she looked up at me with the hint of a smile. "Don't panic Adam, I'm not on the hunt for a boyfriend and we're family now, remember?"

Direct again. "I didn't mean to imply you were, sorry." There it was, sorry again. I was clueless talking to her.

"Don't you have a girlfriend?" she asked me. "Someone called Vanessa?"

I snapped to look at her with surprise. "Who told you that?"

"I can't remember."

"No, we broke up."

"Oh, sorry." It was her turn.

"Coming in?" I asked her.

She shivered. "Ten wetsuits wouldn't get me in the water in this cool weather."

I grinned. "Yeah, well I'm tough, I'll be fine."

She shook her head and I laughed as I tied the leg rope around my ankle, hoisted my board and headed off. As I hit the water, which was bloody cold, I turned back to see Ophelia sitting on the beach near my towel, the dogs standing guard on either side of her. It was nice to have her there, to have a sort of pseudo-family.

~

OPHELIA

I watched Adam and the three other surfers around him. The waves were good and he was pretty good at it. I rose to go back and take Argo and Agnes home for dinner. The sun was almost dipping below the horizon now and would disappear any minute. The ocean was red.

I thought I heard someone whisper my name and I turned, but there was no-one there. That had happened to me a few times, okay, a lot of times in the last week. I wondered if it was Mum or Dad telling me they were with me. It made me shiver even though my jumper was warm enough.

Before Argo, Agnes and I had got halfway home, Adam raced up beside me. He had his towel around his shoulders and board under his arm.

"The temperature drops really quickly once the sun sets," he said.

"You're good on the board."

"Thanks, I love it."

I looked towards our house on the rise. "More lights are on, Uncle Seb must be home."

We walked up towards the path on the beach that led to the house.

"So, did you have a boyfriend in Brisbane?" Adam asked, reversing my former query.

I shook my head. "No."

We got to the path to cross the road, checked for traffic even though it was at the end of a cul de sac and rarely attracted anyone, crossed the road and began the ascent up the driveway, Agnes and Argo rushing up to greet Uncle Seb.

"I've learned a few tricks from being a new kid at school multiple times," Adam said. "Want to hear them?"

"Yeah, oh wise one, sock them to me," I invited him.

"You'll thank me," he teased. "Number one: you shouldn't agree to go out with anyone until you have perspective. Everyone is very nice and likeable when you are new and everyone wants to go out with the new person, but you don't know who they are—whether they are the class idiot or not—and how you feel about anything yet."

"You nailed it," I agreed. "I feel like everyone is watching me and several of the guys have already sort of shown interest, but I don't need that right now and I don't want to make decisions until I feel grounded."

"Good move. To be continued ..." Adam said, and he moved away to the external shower at the side of the house to get the sand off. I opened the front door and Argo, Agnes and I bundled in.

I wondered did he say that to make sure I didn't develop a crush on him. If so, he was either a big head or still in love with Vanessa, whoever she may be.

JACK

I waited for her that night, I waited until five in the morning, just before the sun rose, but she didn't come to the window or join me on the rocks. I'm losing her.

OPHELIA

I had the strangest dream—*a dream within a dream* to quote Edgar Allan Poe, my English teacher would be pleased. I woke up but I was still dreaming. So weird. I dreamt I had always been in this house but I was in the wrong room, and I couldn't find the right room. Even when I woke up, or thought I had woken up, I couldn't work out where I was and I was still searching for my room. I woke up for real sometime after that and realised what was going on. I don't know what it means.

The house howled last night; it wasn't that windy, but I later found out why. Uncle Seb went to bed early; he said he had an early start, but he was quiet and a little flat. The night started normally enough—Mrs Duck had left us a salmon mornay and it was superb. I filled Uncle Seb in on my day and he asked Adam about the injuries he was sporting. Uncle Seb filled us in on his day fighting for funds. Both brutal.

I didn't tell Uncle Seb or Adam about Jack—I don't know why I didn't tell them, they might have known him, but I needed to see Jack again and just wanted to keep him to myself for a while. It had been on my mind all day. There was something about Jack ... something. We sat for a long time not saying anything but his presence was so strong beside me that I missed him when I left him. I've never felt that before.

Anyway, I'm going way off track. After dinner, Argo and Agnes settled onto the rug, Uncle Seb read for a while in the lounge room and I sat opposite him and did my homework. Adam wearing his earphones, sat with his laptop at the kitchen table. I could have gone upstairs, but it was kind of cosy and comfortable downstairs. Regardless, the night dragged on and on ... I just wanted it to be late enough so I could sneak out and see if Jack was there. What if he wasn't there? What if I never saw him again? So what, I told myself a few times. I don't even know him, but I want to know him.

At nine p.m. Uncle Seb rose, kissed the top of my head, then the top of Argo and Agnes's heads, waved goodnight to Adam and turned in. I watched him walk down the hallway, he looked weary. Adam logged out fifteen minutes later and followed suit. I was alone. I went to the window and glanced out—the beach and rocks were deserted.

I returned to the couch, packed away my school gear and put the television on low. I watched a re-run of *Torchwood* just to stop thinking for a while. I nodded off a few times; I'd had so little sleep the night before and was on the rocks with Jack from three o'clock to sunrise, that it was catching up with me.

A loud commercial woke me and I got up and made a hot chocolate. I didn't want to go to sleep too early and risk not seeing Jack. It was then that I discovered what made Uncle Seb a bit melancholy. I was looking through the drawers for a coaster for the table and I found a drawer full of paperwork—insurance papers, how to use the dishwasher manual and a memorial program—I recognised it right away, I had just done one for my parents. It was Meg, his wife's funeral.

I felt someone behind me and turned around, but I was alone; all the hairs on my neck stood up. While I waited for the kettle to boil I read it. Her photo was on the front, she was lovely—athletic, full of life and laughing in the photograph. Inside were tributes and prayers and more photos of her as a child: in a tutu learning ballet, as a lifesaver, a primary school photo, a high school formal shot with a very young Uncle Seb, graduating photos and a beautiful wedding photo of Meg and Uncle Seb. I flicked back to the front page and looked at the date. It was today—today was the anniversary of Meg's funeral. That was why Uncle Seb was melancholy but he didn't say anything. Maybe he didn't want to talk about it or maybe he thought I was carrying enough heavy stuff around.

I ran my finger around Meg's outline and smiled at her. The house howled again; I'm sure it was her. I'm sure she was with Uncle Seb tonight here in the house and I hoped she approved of me. And maybe that's why I dreamt about rooms in the house when I went to bed an hour later. Maybe I'm in her room now and she is displaced.

Before I turned in, I looked outside again but there was no one below on the beach or the rocks. I lay on the bed for a while, listening to the hum of the ocean and the occasional moan of the house. Aside from the dream, I slept right through. When I woke I rushed to the window—it was nearly five-thirty a.m. and no Jack either. I was so tired from the night before that my body just took over and I slept. I was angry at myself and couldn't believe that I would have to wait another twenty-four hours now if he returned to see me. I wonder if he came looking for me last night or if I will ever see him again.

CHAPTER 10

HOLLY

*W*e arrived at Ophelia's place as she was walking down the path to meet us to catch the bus. She sped up and greeted us both. We all waved to Sebastian and the dogs watching from the door.

"Any fights last night?" Ophelia asked.

Harry laughed and told her they didn't happen every day. The bus was coming towards the corner and we sped up to get to the pick-up point. Harry stood back and let Ophelia and I get on board first, he was working on his charm, well, attempting to put on a good show in front of Ophelia anyway.

"Do you think Harry knows Peggy is keen on him?" she whispered as she followed me down the bus aisle.

I grinned and turned back to look at her. "Uh, no. I think it's safe to say Harry doesn't know what day it is."

"I heard that," he said.

"What did you hear?" I asked as he dived into an empty seat on the left-hand side of the bus.

He looked sheepish. "Just my name, but I want to know what you were saying."

Ophelia and I slid into the seat behind him and swapped looks. Ophelia cleared her throat.

"Well, I know someone really lovely, sweet and pretty who likes you," Ophelia set it up.

"Really?" Harry's eyes widened with hopeful anticipation that Ophelia was talking about herself. Like I said, he was clueless.

"Really," Ophelia smiled.

"Well, who?" he grinned.

"Peggy."

His face dropped. "Oh. Well yeah, she's nice I guess."

"She's lovely," I tried to raise her importance. "I heard there are a few guys that like Peggy."

"Yeah?" he seemed curious.

Ophelia tried a different tactic, lowering her voice and leaning forward. "She thinks you're gorgeous and is hoping you will ask her to the dance."

I could see his head swell. "Listen bro, if you want my advice, I'd grab Peggy with both hands. A bird in the hand is better than ... what's the saying... two in the bush or a fish in the tank? Whatever!"

"Yeah great advice, Sis, thanks," Harry smirked. "I'll see what happens ... maybe I'll ask her to the dance.".

I rolled my eyes. "I'm surprised anyone thinks you're gorgeous except Mum," I told him.

"We're identical twins!" he reminded me.

"Not anymore," I twirled a long blond lock of hair around my finger. "Not if I can help it."

Twenty minutes later as the bus stopped outside our school, the senior girls from the back row of the bus walked past and one of them threw a note in Ophelia's lap. She looked up surprised, but the girls kept walking and there was no telling who threw it.

Ophelia grabbed it and looked from me to Harry and back at the note. We got up and followed them out of the bus and into the school grounds.

"What's it say?" Harry looked over Ophelia's shoulders.

She bit her lip as she unfolded it, read it and shook her head. "It says that I'm a slut and I should keep away from Chayse or else."

I put my arm around her shoulder. "Ignore it," I said. "They are friends of Chayse's girlfriend ... the harem."

Ophelia sighed and shoved the note in her shirt pocket. "You know, before my folks died," she stopped as though saying the words took a lot of energy. She continued, "this would have really worried me. But seriously, who cares about this sort of thing. If Imogen or her friends have a problem, they should come and talk with me. I'm not interested in her boyfriend and he's approached me not the other way around."

"I'd say she's threatened," I told Ophelia.

Harry shrugged. "We've got your back, don't worry about it."

Ophelia smiled. "Thanks H and H."

Peggy saw us and rushed over. Harry made a quick getaway.

∼

OPHELIA

Our art teacher's name was Ms Nolan, no relation to the famous painter Sidney Nolan she told us. None of us knew who Sidney Nolan was—okay, Peggy and Christopher Kessels did, but that was about it. She insisted on being called Ms which no one seem to pronounce correctly and every time it sounded like we had said Miss or Mrs she made us say it again.

I liked art. I wasn't very good at it, but I liked the history and the study of words and their meanings. Harry was good, Harry was very good. He could capture faces and expressions, his dimensions and angles worked a treat. As part of our assignment, we had to reproduce a masterpiece. From what I could see, the art world was going to be pretty safe that none of our forgeries was going to flood the market. I picked Picasso's *Weeping Woman*. Everyone thought that was brave, but it was super easy. Everything was a shape and a bright colour and I could cope with drawing a series of triangles ... just.

It was a shame Peggy didn't take art so she could see Harry's work, but she was doing Maths I, Maths II, Science and Physics. I glazed over thinking about it. Ms Nolan glanced over my shoulder, said a few comments about my *Weeping Woman*—I think it might have been an apology to Picasso—and walked on. Holly gave me a grin ... her Jeffrey Smart reproduction wasn't a patch on Harry's work but it was an improvement on mine.

"Oh Harry," Ms Nolan sighed as she walked past him. "Magnificent."

Harry beamed. "Yeah, thanks, Ms Nolan."

Harry was reproducing the *Mona Lisa,* what a ham. Josie Clarke who was painting on the right of me was doing Edvard Munch's *The Scream* and it was positively eerie.

Holly whispered my name and I looked over at her. She had smudged paint on her face and more on her hands than on her apron. She nodded to the window.

I looked out to see Chayse and a group of senior students doing Physical Education—I was a bit slow to discover him out there, most of the girls in the art class were already distracted. Ms Nolan hadn't noticed either. I studied Chayse between my *Weeping Woman* brush strokes. Why was he bothering with me? Did he do that just to rile Imogen or was he genuinely a friendly guy? Or was it to get back at Adam?

It was then I saw Jack—I drew a sharp breath. I had to look twice, but it was definitely him. What was he doing here? He told me he didn't go to school around here but he was sitting in the grandstand in dark pants and the long jacket he'd had on the night I met him. Was he meeting someone else? I moved around my painting closer to Holly.

"See that guy over there sitting in the grandstand?" I whispered to her.

She squinted and looked out at the grounds.

"The cute one in the cute jacket?" she asked.

"Yes. Who is he?" I asked.

She rolled her eyes. "Don't you think you have enough action at the moment? Adam is obviously keen to show you around, Chayse likes you enough to cheese off his girlfriend."

"You know that's so not true," I frowned at her and she looked again. "Do you know him?"

"No," she said, glancing out at him again, "I've never seen him before. Why?"

I shrugged and moved back to my painting. "I saw him on the rocks out the front of Uncle Seb's house the other night."

"Your house," Holly said.

I looked at her. "Yeah, I guess so, my house."

When I looked back, he was gone. I looked around the oval, as far as I could see from my easel but he was nowhere. My heart was pounding. *I'm sorry Jack*, I said in my mind. *I'll be there tonight.* I willed that he might hear me. But what was he doing here? Was he angry that I didn't show last night and was checking up on me? Did he have a girlfriend at this school? I muttered to Holly that I would be back in a minute and asked Ms Nolan if I could slip out to the ladies.

Out in the hallway, I rushed to the exit and squinted in the full light. I tried not to let Chayse or any of his teammates see me. He'd think I was checking him out, yep, just what I needed. I couldn't see Jack, thank God I asked Holly or I would have thought I'd imagined it. I turned to go back in and he was right behind me.

"Jack!" I gasped.

He smiled with that boyish charm, ran his hand through his tasselled sandy-coloured hair and said my name like it was spun gold.

"Ophelia."

Neither of us spoke. I stared into his blue eyes and I felt like he held me in a trance.

"I missed you, I had to see you," he said, then swallowed and looked away. I don't think he wanted to miss me.

My hand went to my heart and I could feel my face blushing. It was a new kind of pain—different from the pain of losing my parents, but still a feeling of separation and I don't know, anticipation maybe.

"I miss you too, Jack," I whispered. "You're taking up all my headspace."

He laughed. "I'm not keeping you up at night though," he said, softening his backhanded insult.

"It's because you kept me up the night before that I couldn't stay awake!" I defended myself. "I'm only human."

"Yes, you are," he said.

I looked into his eyes and saw something there—surprise, trepidation—something unexpected.

"Tonight?" he asked. He didn't touch me despite standing in my space.

Behind me, my name was called and I spun around to see a football hurtling towards me. I flinched and then Jack was there, caught it and returned it just as quickly.

"Got to go," he said and turned the corner of the building before I could say anything. I looked around and I was alone.

Chayse called out. "You okay, Ophelia?"

I nodded and disappeared back into the building. I didn't need the cavalry coming to the rescue. I was back at my easel within minutes.

I could feel Holly looking at me, her hand suspended over her painting, blue acrylic paint on the end of the brush waiting to be applied.

"Are you alright, you look like you've seen a ghost?" she asked.

I nodded. "Fine, just something I ate maybe."

"Or something you didn't," she said. "Lunchtime, you're going to conquer a sandwich!" She turned back to her painting and started dabbing the blue paint into her almost completed sky in the Jeffrey Smart imitation painting.

I sighed. It was nice to have friends that cared but what was Jack doing at my school and how did he get to that football so quickly? Why did I feel like he was reading my soul when no-one else had reached that depth. Freaky.

CHAPTER 11

OPHELIA

*a*dam went to bed first, then Uncle Seb and the dogs—I thought they never would! I watched as eventually, the light spilling out from under their doorways disappeared. I didn't check to see if Jack was there for me on the beach—on our rock—I just wanted to be there. I grabbed my jacket and slipped it around my jeans and pullover. It was a cold night, even chillier when the sea spray hit me. The front door resisted me opening it; Uncle Seb said it swelled and tightened with the salt air. I looked upwards at the ceiling asking for permission and the house gave in and let me out. I quietly closed the door behind me and bolted across the road to the beach.

The cool sand felt wonderful as my toes dug in. I didn't look too far out to sea—the thought of what might lie beneath terrified me. But when it came to meeting Jack, I didn't feel any fear, just the opposite. My heart was playing its own beat, the ocean breeze made me feel alive and awake for the first time in months and soon, he would be here.

Then I saw him. He was sitting on the rock, our rock, where he had led me the first night we met. It looked like he commanded the ocean from there, the moon placed squarely in front of him, the waves lapping the rock in gentle adoration. Then he turned to face me and a slow smile spread across his face. Was he ever in doubt I would come?

JACK

I hated that I needed to see her. I haven't had that before, I've always been in charge and ... well, it doesn't matter, but with her it is different. I sensed it right from the start. I felt her presence before I saw her, and turning, saw she was there watching me. I rose and went down the rock to meet her.

"You came," I said.

She blushed and smiled, her hair floated on the ocean breeze and her eyes were as full as the moon, pale blue, too large for her little face. I extended my hand to her and she placed her hand in mine. I guided her up the rocks to our spot. She was a sure-footed climber, but I felt her eyes boring into me, studying me.

"We won't get washed away here, will we?" she asked with a nervous glance out to sea.

"I hope so," I answered which made her laugh. I read her thoughts then, she agreed. I guess when you lose everything, it takes a while to rejoin the living.

We lowered ourselves to the rock; I didn't let go of her hand. We sat there in silence for a short while, smelling the salt air, feeling the closeness of each other, and how alone we were. It was magic. It was a strange sensation to feel so intensely for someone so quickly. Sure, I've felt attraction before—I thought it was love—but this was different, this was like greed. I was worried about her, I wanted to protect her, keep her ... I just wanted to be with her all the time even if we just stayed here like we were now, forever.

OPHELIA

I couldn't look at him because I desperately wanted to kiss him and I didn't want it to happen too fast ... I want to remember every moment of it. My first kiss, my first real kiss that wasn't Christian McDonald in year eight pinning me against the wall and claiming he loved me.

Without even touching my lips, Jack sucked the air from my lungs, I could barely breath beside him and the chills I felt I was sure weren't from the ocean breeze. I thought I should say something or we might not talk all night, which could be a little weird.

"The waves, that is the tide, it seems higher tonight if that makes sense?" I looked out to sea.

"They are bigger than usual," Jack agreed.

"Why? How is the tide created?" I asked just so I could hear him talk really.

Jack smiled. "Simply put, the earth and the moon are attracted to each other. The moon tries to pull everything on the earth closer, like a magnet. The earth doesn't let it. Except when it comes to water, the earth has trouble holding on to it because it is always moving. So each day the tides rise and fall at the moon's whim I guess you could say."

"That's kind of romantic," I said. Everything was romantic around Jack, I was hopeless.

"We're the earth and the moon, attracted to each other, me pulling you in and hoping you will stay," he teased.

I smiled at him and held his gaze until he broke it. Again, we sat in silence for a while.

"Why were you at my school today?" I asked without looking at him.

He stretched his legs out on the rock in front of him and leaned back, supporting his weight on his arms.

"You don't have to tell me," I shrugged.

"It wasn't another girl," he said.

"I know," I looked at him. I didn't know, but I wasn't going to let on that I would be shattered.

He smiled at me and sat forward again. "I missed you, I told you that."

I frowned. "So you figured if you just showed up and sat on a bench in the grandstand, sometime during the day you might see me?"

"I knew exactly where you were and that you could see me from your classroom," he said as he looked at the ocean then directly at me.

"How?" I asked.

"It doesn't matter."

"Okay," I shut down. We sat again in silence for a while.

"Sorry," he said. "I didn't mean to ... well, I'm out of practice. I wasn't stalking you, I just wanted to see you."

I couldn't help but smile. I wanted that answer. I stammered in my hurry to assure him I felt the same. "I wanted to see you too. I was worried that you might not return." I stopped, I didn't want to say too much and put him off.

He rubbed my hand with his thumb—his hand was so cold—sending a chilled volt through me, but I turned my hand up to wrap my fingers around his. I wanted him to kiss me now, right now. I wanted to feel his fingers on my neck, on my skin, touching my face. I wanted to drink in his kiss in this perfect setting and I would never forget it.

And then he placed his thumb upon my lips, watching me with his deep ocean blue eyes. He moved closer to me, so close I could feel the strands of his hair touching my skin. Could he hear my heart pounding? It was so loud in my ears that it was drowning out my thoughts. All my nerve endings were tingling, my hair full of charge, he was so close to me.

He looked into my eyes.

JACK

I traced her lips, I wanted to kiss her so badly but I wanted this moment to last forever. She sat completely still, her breathing short and sharp, only her eyes moved as she watched my every move. I moved in closer to her.

I suddenly felt weak; she was draining me, not the other way around. How could that be? I looked from her lips into her eyes and I was lost. I closed my eyes to regain my strength; I had to be the one in charge ... what was happening here?

She was so close to me now, her sweet scent overwhelming, I had to kiss her but I was out of control. The power seeped from me into Ophelia, into the ocean, into the rock. I couldn't let it. I swallowed the lump in my throat and forced myself back from her.

A huge wave roared as it crashed against the rock, Ophelia screamed in fright. Did I create it? She leapt up in fear stumbling backwards, but I was up before she lost her footing and I swept her up and charged from the rocks onto safer sand. She wrapped her arms around my neck and buried her face into my shoulder. I could have her now, take her with me, but it was too soon. I wanted more— more of these feelings, was this what life, what love was about? Was this what everyone else got to experience?

I continued to hold her, walking up the sand and hurrying to the entranceway to the beach near her home. I lowered Ophelia to her feet; she was safe now. I touched my hand to her face for just a moment and then slipped away to the nearby rocks, out of sight. I heard her call my name but it was lost just as quickly in the sound of the crashing waves.

CHAPTER 12

HOLLY

*I*t was Friday and everyone was happy about it except Ophelia. You would think given she survived her first few weeks at a new school, the weekend would be the best news she could imagine. She was quiet all the way in on the bus while we all chatted around her. She smiled when addressed and spoke when forced to, but her eyes had a sadness. I wondered if it was maybe her mother or father's birthday or something significant. I asked her if she was okay and she thanked me and said she was good. But she wasn't.

At lunchtime, we sat in a group in the shade of a Lilly Pilly tree. Ophelia leaned against the trunk with her eyes closed.

Harry prodded her. "What's up with you today? Usually, we can't shut you up."

Ophelia grinned. "Yeah, I know it's hard to get a word in around me," she agreed. "I just didn't sleep at all last night. Do you ever get that?"

Peggy nodded. "Sometimes because I don't stop studying until after ten o'clock, I go to bed and my mind is still racing. Takes me ages to drop off."

We all looked at Peggy like she was an alien. Who could relate to that? Good on her though, when we're all struggling to get into university, she'll be knocking them back.

"I hear you," Harry said, "I have that problem all the time." We all laughed and Peggy blushed but still looked pleased to have Harry teasing her.

I agreed with Ophelia. "I woke up one morning at just after two and I was completely wide awake. Not in that sleep zone, half awake, half-dead zone, completely awake! Now that's annoying," I said.

"Yeah, well you've got all weekend to catch up now, I loooovvvvve the weekend," Harry said. "What have you got planned?" he asked Ophelia.

"I could show you around if you like?" Peggy jumped in, probably hoping Harry would come along.

"Thanks, Peggy, you're very kind to offer but Adam is taking me to the site of the La Bella, where his ancestor was a hero. It's for my project," Ophelia said.

"Are you going to dive?" Harry asked.

"No, I haven't done a course, maybe we'll scuba ... I'm kind of happy for him to just stand on shore and point in the general direction," she shrugged.

Harry laughed. "Hey, don't look now but Chayse is heading this way."

We all looked now and it was true—tanned, gorgeous, golden Chayse was walking towards us. Sigh.

Ophelia sat up straight and didn't look happy. He dropped down next to us.

"Hey everyone," he said.

I nodded since I couldn't form a sentence around him and Peggy's mouth just stayed open. Harry grunted a sort of greeting.

"Hi Chayse, do you know my friends?" Ophelia asked and then introduced us before he could answer. He nodded to each of us as she said our names.

"What's up?" she asked.

Before he could answer, one of Chayse's friends came over and sat down as well. This was getting way too weird now. Two of the in-group with us ... why?

"This is Tyler," Chayse flicked his halo head in the new guy's direction. Tyler was tanned and fit too, with a buzz cut and the darkest brown eyes I have ever seen.

"Hey," Tyler answered. Again Ophelia was the only one who found her tongue to greet him. Chayse was gorgeous but Tyler was gorgeous too, not as gorgeous but on a scale of one to ten with Chayse being ten then Tyler was nine. Right, glad we got that sorted. I glanced over to where Chayse's group usually hung out and it is fair to say if looks could kill, we'd all be dead.

Chayse started. "I heard you got a note thrown at you, it was about me."

"It was nothing," Ophelia shrugged.

I found my voice. "We were on the bus on the way to school but we don't know who threw it—it was just a pack of girls, sort of. It said to stay away from you and something else nasty."

Chayse shook his head. "Have you got it?"

Ophelia bit her tongue and thought about it for a few seconds. "It's so not important, really, I'm not worried about it."

Chayse looked frustrated. "I'd like to see it."

She drew a deep breath, opened her bag and pulled it from her pencil case. I don't know why Ophelia decided to keep it, maybe just to remind her of the new school blues. She handed it to him.

"How did you know?" she asked.

"Someone on your bus told me," he said, noncommittally.

He opened the note, frowned and handed it to Tyler who read it and shook his head. He gave it back to Chayse who pocketed it. "This is bullshit," he said. "I'm sorry."

Ophelia blushed. "Really it was nothing, not a big deal. We're cool with it, aren't we?" she turned to us.

"No," I said. "I think it's childish and rude."

"Exactly," Chayse said and gave me a smile. Yeah, a smile just for me with his glorious white teeth and those green eyes looking at me for all of fifteen seconds, okay maybe it was only five seconds before he turned them back to Ophelia.

"Leave this with me Lia, I'll deal with it," he assured her.

She began to protest but he shut her down. "It's not on," he said. "It's just stupid and I'm sorry."

Tyler turned to Harry. "Hey was that a Cell Lapa I saw you riding last weekend?"

"Yeah," Harry looked surprise. "Been saving for it for a while and picked it up a few weeks back. I tell you, the flex-free frame is great, she just begs to be pushed harder. What are you on?"

"A Polygon," Tyler answered.

"Nice," Harry said.

"Yeah, it's a good fit, but I'm thinking of trading up."

Ophelia looked from Tyler to Harry and nudged me.

"What are they talking about?" she whispered.

I rolled my eyes and Chayse grinned.

"Road bikes, you know ... bicycles," I told Ophelia.

"We should go for a spin on Saturday morning. Wouldn't mind trying the Cell if you want to swap for a bit?" Tyler said.

"Sounds good. I'm usually on the road about five," Harry said.

"Five in the morning?" Ophelia exclaimed.

"Some say it's the best time of the day," Chayse teased her.

"Mm, I've gone to bed at that time, but never got up then."

The bell rang and Chayse and Tyler returned to get their bags from their group.

I leaned in. "Can you believe that?"

Peggy shook her head, still with her mouth open, and Harry shrugged indifferently.

Ophelia looked at me confused. "What?" She didn't get that those guys were kings around the school.

Harry rose and pulled us all up, one by one. He's definitely going to charm school—Peggy blushed a deep red. I pulled my uniform down and grabbed my bag.

Ophelia fell in beside me as we walked to our last two classes for the day.

"Lia, I can assure you," I began, "before you arrived, Chayse and Tyler wouldn't know we existed, let alone come over and talk to us."

She shrugged. "Maybe they just didn't have a reason to before."

Sometimes, I don't think Ophelia realises the amount of attention she has circling her orbit.

∾

OPHELIA

I am in agony. I walked up the path to my house—my house, there I said it—and I was so relieved to say goodbye to everyone and be alone. I guess the distraction today was good but I just need to think. I opened the front door and the lovely Argo and Agnes sensed my despair and sidled up to me. I gave them both a big hug. I had the house to myself, well people-free anyway. I grabbed a Diet Coke from the fridge, went up the stairs, threw my bag into my room and continued up the stairs to the attic. Agro and Agnes came with me and we sat in front of the large windows looking out to sea.

Why did he leave without saying something, without kissing me? Did he change his mind? Did I turn him off or say something wrong? I replayed it in my head all day, a thousand times—touching my lips, scooping me up and racing down the rock so in charge, so confident in his movements. Then he moved away slightly and rubbed his eyes. He touched my cheek for just a minute, his hand was icy cold, and then he was gone. Why? What was he seeing that I wasn't?

All through art class, I kept looking out for him, but he didn't come. Unbearable, I'm an idiot making myself sick over him.

It's Friday night, will he come tonight? Who is he with tonight? Why, Jack? Why have I done this to myself?

I've been here a minute and instead of mourning my folks, I'm losing my head, or heart, to someone I only just met and now I am in twice as much pain. I'm seriously stupid. I stood up and paced, sat down again and then rose and paced again, clueless as to how it went so quickly from almost kissing me to running away from me.

He said he missed me, I just reciprocated. Maybe telling him what was in my head was too much. God, I'm such an idiot. I closed my eyes and took several deep breaths.

He might come tonight. Maybe I should just join my parents ... I could be buried at sea. Not a healthy thought, but I didn't have many bright thoughts at the moment.

CHAPTER 13

ADAM

She wasn't happy about something—maybe it was a bad day at school or after the first few weeks, it was all just a bit overwhelming. We both noticed it—Sebastian and I—and we discussed it after she turned in early last night, really early especially for a Friday night. Around midnight Seb went up to check on her but she wasn't in her room. He saw her in the attic seat watching the beach but didn't invade her space. Kind of hard to know whether to interfere or not, but she might have wanted some time out to think … about her parents, school, whatever was in her head. None of us was good communicators.

Next morning, I glanced over at Ophelia as we pulled out of Seb's garage and began our drive to Warrnambool together. We were both rugged up—it was a cold morning. We would be back from the wreck site just after lunch or earlier if she didn't want to eat. I bit my lip, while deciding whether to raise it with her or not. Our communication to date hadn't been great, she was direct, I was tactless. What the heck.

"You okay?"

She looked over at me and smiled. "Sure, how are you?"

"Yeah, I'm fine," I rolled my eyes. "But you're not."

She sighed and looked away.

"Okay, dropping it," I said.

"Good," she turned to look at me. "How long will it take to get there?"

"About twenty minutes. Why? You want out already?"

She rolled her eyes and smiled again. "No Mr Paranoid, I just like to have my bearings. So, since you've got a captive audience, tell me about your relative who became a hero."

"Ah, yes, runs in the family," I said to get a laugh and it worked.

"Go on you big ham," she encouraged me.

I headed towards the Highway and drawing a deep breath began my tale.

"My ancestor, a very handsome young man lived and worked in Warrnambool and he was in the right place at the right time, not to mention he was phenomenally brave when a shipwreck went down. Still with me?" I asked.

"Yeah, it's hardly complex yet. A lot different from Chayse's storytelling," she added.

"Mm, yeah that would have been a dry telling," I took my eyes off the road to momentarily glance at her. She only mentioned that to get back at me for my last wisecrack, I'm sure.

"Go on," she said.

It felt nice to have her beside me … to be friends with a girl and enjoy each other's company without all the other tension and drama.

I continued: "La Bella was a Norwegian-built ship, a barquentine —that's a sailing vessel with three or more masts—quite beautiful."

"I saw a picture of her in the library when I started my assignment," she said.

I nodded. "Seb's got a model of her in his study. Well, La Bella was approaching Warrnambool with a load of timber. She'd come from New Zealand. The seas were really rough and there was a mist too. It was November 1905 and the captain, Captain Mylius ordered the ship steer for the light, as you would. But as it came around, she was hit by a really rough sea."

I saw her shudder and she rubbed her arms.

"Cold?" I asked, reaching to adjust the air conditioning.

"No," she assured me. "It's just that I was on the rock when a huge wave hit and it just roared. Scared me half to death, so I can't imagine what it would be like being out in a ship in a roaring sea."

"I know. While I've been surfing, I've had some huge waves that pinned me to the bottom of the ocean and I thought it was all over. The sea is a harsh mistress," I said.

"Mm, what's that from?" she asked.

"So you're saying I couldn't come up with a line like that?"

She laughed again.

I was good for her, I'm sure. "Okay, some poet," I agreed.

"Oh well, that narrows it down," she made fun of me, again. She was winning. "Please, continue."

"Ah yes, La Bella. The huge, treacherous ocean struck her, knocking her around, waves breaking over her, until she was literally thrown on to a submerged reef."

"Ouch," Ophelia winced.

"I know. You can almost hear the grinding of the reef on the ship's bottom, can't you? So, the Warrnambool Harbour Master, whose name was Captain Roe—but spelt Roe not row—and four lifesavers rowed out in a whaleboat to help. Most of the usual lifeboat crew were away and so volunteers were called in," I stopped for breath.

"And this is where your great, great, great ..."

"Grandfather volunteered," I finished her sentence. "The other volunteers got the whaleboat out but it was pretty impossible to get near the La Bella because of the breakers. The rescue went on for about ten hours but the lifeboat crew couldn't get close enough to the ship and were forced to return to shore. The sailors got weaker and were suffering from exposure and exhaustion, and a few got washed overboard."

"So terrifying," she shuddered again.

I stopped talking for a moment to negotiate some traffic and we continued on. "So, three of the men were eventually rescued and my relative, William Ferrier sculled out twice in a small dinghy and saved two others including Captain Mylius. The rest of the La Bella crew of twelve were washed overboard. The captain was suspended for twelve months and William was awarded twenty pounds and a silver medal," I finished on a high.

"One of the drowned men was Chayse's ancestor then?" I asked.

"Yeah, Pierre Johann was his name. He didn't make it. Neither did the captain in the long run. It's said that the stress caused him to have a heart attack six months after the incident; he never sailed again and died at age thirty-seven."

"Poor man, I can only imagine. And the wreck is still there, that's where we're going," she stated.

I nodded. "She lies on her port side in the sheltered water inside the reef she struck. This bow section is relatively intact and the reef where she struck is now called La Bella reef."

"I wonder why more people didn't do what William did, you know grab a boat and help," she said.

"Too risky. He seemed like a pretty humble guy though—there's a record somewhere of his thank-you speech and he says 'I only tried to do my duty, and I am sure that every man ... would have done as much',"[1] I said in my best imitation of delivering a speech.

"It was heroic," she agreed. "I couldn't do it. Could you?"

I frowned. "I don't think any of us really know unless we're tested."

OPHELIA

I was relieved to spend the day with Adam. It was nice sitting beside him, watching him handle the drive so effortlessly, taking charge and distracting me for a while.

I had a bad night—Jack didn't show. I don't know why or where he is. I wish I had never met him. I found myself moving from the aching pain to the anger stage.

I'm just going to have friends from now on, like Adam and the twins, Peggy, Argo and Agnes. Just trust in Uncle Seb and keep life simple for a while.

Adam turned into the Warrnambool breakwater area. It was so beautiful and weird to be constantly surrounded by water here and at home. In my former life, the only time I saw coastal water was the annual Christmas holiday to the Gold Coast for a week. Now I was surrounded by more water than land. He pulled his white four-wheel-drive into a car park next to a ute and small sedan.

I thanked him and we got out. I removed my camera from my backpack and threw the strap over my shoulder. Adam grabbed a jacket for me which I offered to carry, but he said he had it under control. Good thing the cars were parked away from the jetty as the waves and sea spray crashed against it with a loud slap.

"The dive boats go from the Lady Bay boat ramp," Adam said pointing to a ramp in the distance. "We can hire a boat and just go over the top, the wreck is about thirteen metres below the water so you're not going to see it but you can get an idea of where it lies. Or I can just show you from here."

It was really rough out there, I mean really rough. He must have read my mind and said, "come on, we'll have a look at the general area."

I nodded, pleased. We walked around the area while Adam indicated where the La Bella came in, where it ran into trouble, and where the wreck now lay. I took photos of the area and took it all in. It was amazing to think that a piece of history lay below the surface of the water. If I wasn't such a scaredy-cat I would have loved to have dived below to see it ... maybe one day. I could tell Adam was itching to get into a boat and go out, even to drift over the top of it.

"Sorry to be such a landlubber," I shrugged. I wondered if he was disappointed in me—I hated to be a wet blanket.

Adam laughed. "It's pretty wild out there today, let's not tempt fate."

"Are you referring to the curse, the myth I mean?" I asked.

He looked surprised. He dug his hands into his jeans pockets and looked at me quizzically.

"Who told you about that?"

"Everyone when I started doing this assignment."

"Mm," he said. "It's just superstition."

I nodded. "So do you go out after midnight?"

"Not if I can avoid it," he said.

~

ADAM

We left the La Bella wreck area and I took Ophelia to see some of the best swimming and surfing beaches.

I couldn't believe it—when we headed further down the beach, guess who was there? Yep, Chayse Johann. Every other day he's surfing at Port Fairy when I'm there, but no today, he decides to surf near his home. The guy's a dick.

He sees Ophelia, waves, drops the board and has the nerve to come over. Glad to see he's still sporting a few cuts and bruises since we last met.

"Hey Ophelia," he says, then looks at me and says my name, "Adam."

"Chayse," I expelled his name between gritted teeth.

"What are you doing here?" he asks Ophelia. He's standing there wet from the ocean in just his boardies, no wetsuit in this cold, and thinking he's some surf legend.

Ophelia looks to me. "Adam is helping me with my assignment, so we're checking out the area where La Bella lies and just doing some tourist sightseeing."

"Yeah, well check out the facts too," Chayse said.

"What's that supposed to mean?" I arced up. I felt Ophelia's hand go to my chest and she gently pushed me back a step.

"I'm doing plenty of research," she assured him. "You've both been really helpful." Ophelia steered the subject onto something safe and looking out to sea, said: "surf looks good."

"Yeah you should get back to it," I suggested.

Chayse ignored me.

"Want me to take you out in the boat?" he asked Ophelia.

I step forward again. "What a good idea since clearly that wouldn't have occurred to me," I snapped.

He glared at me and Ophelia physically moved in front of me.

"Ah, thanks Chayse, but we've got it covered. In fact, we were just leaving, right Adam?"

Chayse and I were too busy staring each other down for me to answer.

"Right, Adam?" she said a little louder. "Bye, Chayse, good to see you." She turned, hooked her arm through mine and led me away.

"Yeah see you Lia, catch you Monday at school."

I'm catching her right now, tonight and all day Sunday too, buddy, I thought. I sighed. Why did I let that idiot get to me? I looked down at Ophelia and she had the trace of a smile upon her lips.

I rolled my eyes. "I know, sorry. It's just he's a ..."

"Yeah, I get it," she cut me off.

"I'm starved. Want to eat?" I asked.

"A coffee at least," she agreed. She reeled around quickly to stare at someone.

"What's up?" I asked and looked to see what had distracted her.

She abruptly turned away and looked to the distance.

"Nothing, I just thought I saw someone ... something," she shook her head.

I could swear her eyes filled with tears but she turned her face from me and when I next glanced, she was back under control. We headed back to my car, I unlocked it and taking her camera, put it and her jacket that I had been carrying in the back. As we were driving away I could see Chayse putting on a show for her; further along the beach lay Imogen with her girlfriends, sunning themselves despite the cold.

"He's got a gorgeous girlfriend, why's he hanging around you?" I said without thinking, again.

She looked at me and grimaced. "Yeah, why would you hang around me ... unattractive, anaemic-looking me, when you have Imogen?"

I shook my head. Too late to take that back, I began back-peddling fast.

"I didn't mean that. You're gorgeous too, but ... and I mean in a sisterly way ... but I'm just saying when is enough going to be enough for that guy?" I glanced at her and realised I was only making it worse. "I'll shut up."

"Are you sure you want to be seen with me for coffee? You could do better," she asked.

Crap ... this was all Chayse's fault again. I drummed my fingers on the steering wheel, my mind working overtime on how to dig myself out of this one. I turned the car towards the cafe on the foreshore with the beautiful ocean view—that should impress her.

She punched my arm and grinned.

"Lighten up, Adam, I'm only playing you."

I breathed a sigh of relief. "I can't tell," I told her. "We don't know each other well enough for you to play me yet."

"Well get used to it, bro," she said with the emphasis on "bro".

I pulled over into a car park out in front of the cafe.

"My shout," I said, "since I'm the working one and the one who has to make amends."

"Least you could do," she agreed, with a smile. "C'mon, I'll see if I can spot someone who is your type. You should call me sis though, just so that no one thinks you're stuck with me."

"Yeah, yeah," I grimaced. I guess I deserved that one.

CHAPTER 14

JACK

I knew she was in pain, so was I. It was made worse for me by the fact that she was hanging around with Adam and that Chayse guy—both of them looking out for her. When she put her hand on Adam's chest I nearly tore between them. I felt my heart rip with jealousy.

I'm trying to keep away from her, but she's not like the others. I was in control and when it was over with them, that was it. But she's got some power over me—she wants me but doesn't need me; she drains from me and it makes her stronger. How is she doing that or am I doing it because I've been blindsided by her?

I watched her the morning I took her home, holding her in my arms and carrying her up the beach. She lay in bed after, tossing and turning in those few hours before dawn. I followed her to school and watched her in art class ... her eyes always outside, seeking me. I wanted to stop the pain for both of us and just appear, but I have to think this through. If she is stronger than me, I may have to give her up or never let her see me, she'll destroy me. But I don't think I could watch her with someone else.

She waited for me all Friday night, sitting in the attic window—a pale, lonely figure. I wanted to go to her and to kiss and hold her so badly I ached. I hate this.

No, it's best I stay away. I'm trying to stay away.

Can you stay away from your destiny?

OPHELIA

Monday. I never, ever thought I would be pleased to have a Monday school morning thrust upon me but I need to get out of my head. I just need to be busy, be with my new friends and not think about him.

No sighting of him, no sign of him. He's gone—I don't know what I was to him, but it is over, as brief and intense as it was.

I hate you, Jack.

Don't come back, don't come near me. For you to let me hurt like I have since dawn Friday morning ... to not come to me or even explain ... you have no heart.

I am not thinking about you anymore.

I am not going to waste any more of my life on you Jack. I don't know why we clicked anyway... maybe because we were alike; maybe because you just got me and didn't feel sorry for me or see me as the new girl.

I sighed, you're out Jack! If only my heart could fall in sync with my head and do what I asked.

HOLLY

"You will never believe it," I said to Ophelia as we hurried for the bus.

"What?" she asked.

"It's here, hurry up," Harry said going ahead of us to wave the bus down before we all missed it. Ophelia and I raced behind him.

We got on board and I glanced to the pack of girls that had thrown the threatening letter at Ophelia. They were glaring at us, well at Ophelia. She didn't seem to notice. We dropped into our customary seats halfway down the bus and Harry turned around and leaned over the seat.

"Good weekend?" he asked Ophelia.

"Yeah, thanks. Adam took me around and showed me some of the sites for the assignment," she answered.

"Lucky duck," I sighed. "I wish Adam would show me around the sights, any sights, the local tip would do!"

Ophelia laughed and then looked glum again. I don't know what's going on with her. I wonder who she was before she came here, you know, what she was like when her life used to be normal, with parents and everything. She still looked pale and tired to me, more than she did when she first arrived.

"Hey did you and Tyler go cycling?" she asked Harry.

"Yeah," Harry said acting casual. "We swapped bikes and then did a good long circuit. We're going to do it again next weekend."

Ophelia looked pleased, so did Harry even if he was trying to be cool about it. He continued to prattle on about the weekend and I scolded him.

"Shh, I've got news for Lia."

"Sorry, sorry," Ophelia remembered I was about to tell her something. "You were saying ... what won't I believe?"

Harry rolled his eyes and sat back. "Go ahead with your girls' talk." But I noticed he still listened in. Behind us, someone yelled as a rowdy game of throwing someone's bag around got a bit out of hand.

"What won't I believe?" Ophelia pushed.

I lowered my voice and leaned in closer. "I saw on Facebook that Imogen and Chayse have broken up."

Ophelia looked surprised. "Really?" she said. "They were on the beach together on Saturday."

Harry shrugged. "Must have happened after that. Who cares?"

"I care," I declared. "Because I think he's keen on Lia."

"No way," she said. "Besides I'm busy. I've got school and a project, study, you guys, Peggy, Uncle Seb, Adam and the dogs to manage, I'm busy."

I rolled my eyes and sat back. "You're the only girl in the whole school and probably the whole planet who would be too busy for Chayse Johann."

Ophelia laughed. "Whole planet? Wow!"

I grinned, "Too much? Okay just here then." I watched as she cast a furtive glance to the back of the bus.

∼

OPHELIA

Peggy and I sat side-by-side in the library working on our history projects. What I loved about Peggy was that she was wonderfully oblivious to drama, and she loved Harry. She didn't ask about Adam, didn't moon over Chayse, and had no idea he had broken up with Imogen. She probably didn't know he was going out with Imogen. But she knew plenty of other stuff.

"Are you going to join a club?" she leaned over and asked.

"I hadn't given it much thought," I said. I hadn't given it any thought actually.

"I know what you're thinking," she continued. "You're thinking there's so many and how do you fit them in with homework and study."

I nodded. I was happy to run with that thought.

"What are you going to join?" I asked.

"I'm already in the music club, and the book club, but I'm thinking … actually, Dad's pressuring me to join a club with some physical activity in it," she shuddered as she said it.

"We could join one of those together," I suggested. It was the least I could do for Peggy who had looked after me so well. "I hear there's a tri-club … we could make up a team of three … you know one of us does the run, the other the swim and the other the cycle?"

"I don't know but we can ask," Peggy said. "Ooh, I love that idea, Lia, thanks. Dad will be rapt. You know, Harry was the cross country champion for Year 10 last year but he likes to cycle too." She brightened. "We could ask him to join our tri team and he could do the cycling leg unless you wanted to do that of course?" She looked at me with worried eyes, keen to have Harry in our team.

I grinned; this was getting better all the time. "Nope, I'm a runner but I can swim if absolutely necessary."

Peggy breathed a sigh of relief. "That's perfect because I'm good in the pool, not so good on land."

"We've got the perfect team—tick that box then," I whispered, noticing the librarian glancing our way. "Let's suss it out later."

Peggy smiled enthusiastically and moved back to continue her assignment. I looked at the clock; I hadn't thought of Jack for twenty minutes. What a great distraction Peggy was. I returned my attention to going through the digitised old newspaper about La Bella in the Trove archives. It was surreal to be able to read the newspaper extracts from 1905 when it actually happened.

I scanned the newspapers; the first news story I could find was from *The Argus* on 16 November 1905 saying "no bodies have since been found."[1] Gruesome! Next was a notice on Friday 29 November in the *Geelong Advertiser* that "the conduct of the lifeboat crew was in every way satisfactory, that they had done everything possible to save the wrecked sailors, and that even if the regular lifeboat crew had been on board he did not think they could have done any more.

He spoke highly of Fisherman Ferrier's conduct, but pointed out that he in his dinghy could go where the lifeboat could not.[2]

You go Adam's great, great, great grandfather! Next were a few tiny lines in the *Colac Herald* on Friday 29 December that read: "Captain Mylius has been remanded at Sydney to Melbourne on a charge of manslaughter.[3]

And then I saw it ... a picture or rather a drawing of the deceased men who lost their lives on the La Bella; some of them not much older than me.

I reeled back in fright. I couldn't believe it. I leaned in closer to the screen again. The last man on the far right of the picture was my Jack... Jack Denham.

CHAPTER 15

OPHELIA

*T*he picture waited in my school bag, throbbing in my consciousness, but I didn't look at it again until after dinner. I excused myself telling Uncle Seb and Adam that I had to do an assignment and was going to do it in my room. They both looked worried, so I tried to look as cheery as possible, even though my stomach was churning and I knew upstairs, pressed in my history book was a photo of a dead guy I was in love with. I'm seriously weirded out.

I entered the room and before I turned on the lights I grabbed the curtains, hiding behind them as I slid them closed. I had spent the last four days watching the rocks and the beach for Jack, now I didn't want to risk seeing him. I turned on a lamp and dropped onto the end of the bed. What do I do with this information? Jack is in a photo dated 1905. Even though it is a grainy, brown photo I know it's Jack, he's even wearing the same jacket he wears now. How can this be? Is he a ghost? There's no such things as ghosts, well there might be, who knows, I mean how would I know if there are ghosts or not. I saw him in the daytime, you can't see ghosts in the daytime. Can you?

I grabbed my laptop and opened it. I searched for ghost

characteristics ... maybe there's an expert on ghosts. Ghost hunters, ghost chasers, paranormal experts, close encounters of the ghost type ... that will do nicely. I opened the page and scrolled down until I found ghost characteristics. Okay, deep breath. I began to read: a ghost can appear day and night but appearing at night is much easier as there is less interference. What sort of interference? Doesn't matter. Appearing during the day drains a new ghost but old ghosts are capable of living amongst us undetected day and night. If Jack is a —sounds insane—ghost then he would be an old ghost, well over a hundred years old. I saw him and talked to him during the day, he would be strong enough to do that. It also explains how he got to that football so quickly and lifted me off the rocks. Have I been picked up by a ghost, literally? I read on and couldn't believe what I was reading. A ghost can completely resemble a human and get stronger if love is reciprocated!

I sat back and thought about it. If Jack wanted to get stronger, why wouldn't he want my love? Why did he reject me? I went back to the list. Next, they can charm a human to fall for them—yeah, no shit. They can appear or disappear—well that kind of explains how he disappeared on the beach that morning when he deserted me. The next one made sense; a ghost needs heat energy to manifest, so the air around them grows colder. I felt that around him and his hands were so cold too.

I heard a knock at the door and I put the laptop down and went to answer it. Adam was standing there in track pants and T-shirt, brandishing two cups of hot chocolate.

"Seb and I thought you might need a chocolate fix?" he said.

I stood aside and let him in.

"Want me to leave this and go?" he asked.

"No, drink with me," I invited him. Delaying discovering about Jack the ghost for half-an-hour wouldn't make much difference.

He passed me the cup of hot chocolate and moved to the window.

"Can I open the curtains?" he asked.

"No!" I didn't mean to say it quite so loudly.

"Right," he looked at me suspiciously and lowered himself into a chair. "You want to tell me what's going on? Maybe I can help."

"No." I moved to the end of the bed, turned the laptop away from him and sat down. I sipped my hot chocolate trying to think of a new conversation topic.

"No you don't want to tell me, or no you don't think I can help?"

"Don't ask me," I muttered. "Not yet."

He nodded. "Just tell me, does it have anything to do with Chayse Johann?"

I shook my head. "Absolutely nothing ... promise."

He seemed satisfied with that answer. Adam looked back at the closed curtains and then at me.

"Has something spooked you?"

I shook my head.

"Is someone following you or watching you?"

I shook my head again.

"Has ..."

"Adam! Have you finished your hot chocolate yet?" I asked. Clearly he didn't get the real meaning of 'don't ask me'.

He laughed. "Right, sorry, I'll take the hint. Not much of a hint, more like a smack across the head. So I'm off." He rose and headed for the door, turning as he reached it. "I mean it though Lia. If I can help ..." he turned and left.

When I was sure that he had truly departed, I put the hot chocolate down and sat back on the bed. I turned the laptop and read the last of the ghost traits listed on the site—ghosts remain the age they were when they died. So Jack was seventeen when he died, he's seventeen now but he looks older—maybe because in those days, men started work in their teens and women were married and became mothers when they were super young, so they grew up quicker and looked more mature.

Reading on: ghosts don't have a requirement for sleep like humans, they are restless creatures without a shadow. If the ghost is a

111

demon, something will be missing when they take human form. I cringed ... major creepy! But Jack was one hundred per cent there, I was sure of it. I could feel his presence so strongly and he took my hand, he carried me. That's good; he's probably not a demon then. I looked at the photo again; it was definitely Jack.

I was torn. I needed more information and I knew just the person to talk with—Uncle Seb. I looked at the large clock hanging near the door. It was ten-thirty and Uncle Seb was usually in his study until late; I had to see if he was up.

I grabbed my empty hot chocolate cup and made my way down the stairs. The lounge room was in darkness, as was the kitchen. I didn't put on the lights, just made my way to the sink with the moonlight provided, avoiding looking out the windows, which took all my will power. I was too frightened of what I might see; I was frightened he might appear but I wanted him to as well.

Argo and Agnes had turned in, but Uncle Seb's light was still on down the hallway. I coughed lightly as I walked down the hallway so I didn't startle him.

"Is that you, Adam?" he called.

"No, it's me Uncle Seb," I appeared in his doorway.

He sat behind his desk, wearing his glasses and working on a model ship.

"Lia," he smiled and removed his glasses. "What's up?"

"Can I talk to you about the La Bella?" I asked.

"Of course, you know I'll talk about ships until the ships come in ..." he smiled at his own joke. "Take a seat." He looked around and pointed to a ship model with its rows of sails up. That's her there," he said.

I pulled up a chair on the other side of his desk.

"She's beautiful. I was wondering what you knew about the crew?" I asked. "For my assignment."

"Ah yes, how's that going?" he asked.

"Great. I'm looking at a number of shipwrecks, but Chayse and Adam have both helped with the La Bella stuff and I've got some good information from the news clippings. There's not much about the crew—those who died and survived." I added both to avoid suspicion.

Uncle Seb nodded. "There's a photo of William Ferrier with some of the survivors."

"I saw it," I said, "and one image of some of the victims."

"Yes, there's little recorded about the deceased," Uncle Seb said. "It was a terrible end—the exhaustion, the conditions, trying to hold on and some of them only lads."

He opened his own files and notes about the local area. He showed me several photographs and spoke about the survivors. I waited patiently not wanting to give away my urgency. Finally, he started talking about those who didn't make it. Just get to Jack!

"Then there was a young sailor Jack Denham, seventeen years old." Uncle Seb turned to his computer and opened a file—he had a press clipping that I hadn't seen. He read aloud parts of it to me about when a gigantic wave shocked onlookers and made survival seem impossible: "It seemed certain that the crew could no longer retain their precarious hold. To the amazement and the relief of the awestricken spectators, the plucky fellows still held on, but shortly after they were compelled to remove to a higher portion of the vessel, which had swerved right over on her beam ends, and began to gradually disappear."

I thought of Jack clinging for life and realised how much more real the tragedy seemed to me now. Uncle Seb read on: "The unfortunate men on the schooner could be seen from shore piteously imploring the lifeboat to come nearer ... the sufferers whose lives were hanging in the balance ... could perceptibly feel the ship slowly sinking beneath them." Uncle Seb stopped and looked at me. "You sure this won't give you nightmares Lia?" he asked.

"It probably will Uncle Seb," I realised I had my hand on my heart while I was listening to him read the account. "But it's history."

"That it is," he agreed.

"Please keep going, I haven't come across this information yet," I said leaning forward and wrapping my arms around myself for warmth and support.

He nodded and read on. My ears were listening for Jack's name and then he read it. "The first mate, Coulson, had his leg broken by falling debris, and he and the boy [Jack] Denham were washed away together at a later stage, in consequence of releasing their hold through their hands becoming benumbed."

Jack's hands were so cold. He must have held on for as long as he could, until he could no longer feel his hands or feel them releasing the rope.

Uncle Seb read what information he had, finishing with a note about Jack: "he was the youngest on board and originally from Melbourne." He strolled down the news clipping and read the captain's statement: "Denham was too exhausted to move when the others charged to the starboard bow, and soon afterwards disappeared."

I blinked away tears before Uncle Seb could notice.

"From memory, I'm pretty sure they found his body though," Uncle Seb said.

"Did they?" I leaned forward.

"Let me see," he rifled through press clippings saved on his computer. "Yes here. Ah well, they sort of found his body." He read the clipping. "This is from *The Advertiser*, 24 November 1905: 'at the inquest to-day on the headless body found yesterday, it was stated that the body was believed to be that of the boy, Jack Denham, who was washed off the wrecked vessel. The funeral took place this afternoon, and was attended by the survivors from the wreck and a number of residents of Warrnambool'[1]. That's it. Although I remember from my readings that there was some initial confusion as to whether the body was Jack's or seaman Harry Watson."

"Where do you think Jack is buried, if it is Jack?" I asked.

"I believe he is buried in the Warrnambool cemetery—you might find the cemetery records online."

"If he was from Melbourne, I wonder why his family didn't take him back there to bury him," I thought out loud.

"Perhaps he had no family or they didn't have the money to do that. It was a different time," Uncle Seb reminded me. "In those days, often people were buried where they died. They didn't have the preservation methods like they do now to keep the body cold and stored for days on end."

"Creepy, again. Thank you, Uncle Seb," I rose. "I know it's getting late, I don't want to keep you up."

"Anytime Lia," he said pulling off his reading glasses again. "I hope that helps."

"You've been a huge help," I assured him, gave him a kiss goodnight on his cheek and I re-entered the dark hallway. I headed up the stairs to my room. I had to go to the cemetery.

CHAPTER 16

JACK

She knows, Ophelia knows about me and yet, she's not scared. I was there when Sebastian was telling her of my death and I felt her sadness and compassion for me; I knew she was different. But I still don't know why she is stronger than the others and why being with her might be the end of both of us.

I've had a lot of time to think over the last few days as I watched her grow to resent and hate me, and miss and love me. If I can keep my power long enough to take Ophelia with me to my world, I don't care then if it is the end for both of us—we'll be together forever.

She can at least sleep; hours of the day wiled away in unconsciousness while I am awake every minute of every hour of every day trying not to think of her.

It is supposed to be getting easier but it is not. I can't bear thinking of her with another guy, his hands upon her, his lips on her mouth—I can't stand it!

OPHELIA

I returned to my room and closed the door. I sank down to the floor, leaning against the bed. After Mum and Dad had died I thought I had no tears left to cry but I was wrong; hearing how Jack had died, so cold, and after a struggle was devastating. Is that why he couldn't move on ... because his life never really had a chance to start?

I rose from the floor, I was going to right this. I don't care what Jack is or what Jack was, he's here now and I want to know why, and why he shunned me.

I strode to the curtains and pulled them open. Standing on our rock silhouette by the moon was Jack; his hands in his coat pockets, his head held high. He was looking directly at the window—at me, the first time he had appeared in a week. I wasn't going to let him off lightly. I held his gaze and he stared back.

"Come to me, Jack," I whispered. A dark cloud passed in front of the moon and the beach was cloaked in darkness. When the moon seeped out again he was gone.

"No, Jack!" I cried with anger.

"I'm here," a voice said behind me and I spun around.

I breathed heavily; he took the air from the room standing there behind me.

"Ophelia," he said my name and stepped towards me.

I shook my head. "Don't you dare, Jack, don't ..."

He looked away from me, and out the window to the ocean. He drew a deep breath and the room chilled.

"You're strong, you take my power from me," he said, returning his gaze to me. "You'll destroy me, but I need you like you need oxygen."

I stepped back and shook my head. "No Jack. You left me ... you didn't come ..."

"It was a mistake," he stepped towards me and I put my hands up to stop him. He stayed where he was, his eyes boring through me. "Are you ... scared of me?"

"No," I said.

"You know what I am, Ophelia. I would have told you, eventually."

"I'm not scared of you," I said. I noticed my hands were shaking and I folded my arms in front of me. I moved away from the window.

I shook my head. "You don't get it, Jack. I ..." I couldn't say I was in love with him aloud. It was too early, too wrong, too right. And if he freaked out last time just because I said he was in my head ...

"I am in your head, in your space, in your bedroom, in your world," he said reading my thoughts. "I didn't leave Ophelia because I didn't want you, I left because I had no right to ... possess you."

I couldn't breathe, the room was cold and Jack was so close and I was trying to think about every word he said and what it meant and if he was coming back to me, when he rushed towards me.

"No!" I tripped backward and pushed him away. "I don't trust you ... I'm better now, I've forgotten you."

He scoffed.

"I have," my eyes flared in defiance as I backed up to the bedroom door. I felt for the doorknob. "You don't get to just walk back into my life when it suits you. I'm not your on-and-off beach buddy."

"Listen to me," he tried to placate me.

"You have nothing I want to hear, Jack," I said. His face fell and he bit his tongue, looking at me. He was close enough to reach me, but kept his distance.

I continued. "I know who you are, or who you were, and I am so, so very sorry about what happened to you. But you just go on, I don't. I can't do much more heartbreak ... not this month, maybe not this year." I could feel myself tearing up again. Damn.

Jack at least looked ashamed.

"Believe me, I didn't disappear from your world because I didn't care," he said again. "Ophelia, I have drowned once before, but you were drowning me again. I don't know what it means yet, I've never felt that."

The house moaned loudly. I had to get out of the room, it was so cold and if I stayed, I knew I would forgive him. I turned the doorknob quietly behind my back while he spoke and swung around quickly to leave.

Jack was there, he slammed the door closed, locked it and spun me around.

"Forgive me?" he pressed against me.

I used my anger like a shield over my heart. He wouldn't get the chance to hurt me twice. I struggled to get away from him.

"Don't fight me, Ophelia, you drain us both," he said. "Stop, please."

He pressed so hard against me I couldn't move. I wanted to kiss him so badly.

"Please Ophelia," he whispered.

I stopped and let the fight escape my body. He pressed his forehead against mine and I closed my eyes and gripped him in case he disappeared.

JACK

Her touch was burning me, draining me and yet she shivered from my cold presence.

She drew ragged breaths and if I had been alive, my heartbeat would have been matching the fast drumbeats I could hear from her heart.

"You're killing me, but being away from you is killing me more," I whispered to her. I moved back only a little, enough to see her face fully. She was so fragile and beautiful; those huge eyes looking up at me with no fear. I had to kiss her this time.

My lips touched hers and I breathed her in. She returned my kiss, my first kiss that really mattered. She pulled away and her hand reached for my face, the warmth seeping through me, the power leaving my body. She touched my face with curiosity.

"Don't do that to me again, Jack," she said. "Be with me or don't, but don't leave me hanging."

"You know what I am now," I looked into her eyes. "It is your decision, Ophelia. I can't pretend I am good for you, that I can give you any sort of life ..."

"Shh," she pressed her finger to my lips. "Times have changed since 1905. Men don't need to provide for women any more, Jack. Having you, us ..."

"You don't know what you're saying yet," I told her. "I'll show you, soon, what a life with me would be like. Once you truly know, if you can't be with me, then I will understand and leave, forever. I won't put you through anything like this again. You can keep my old photo and maybe, every now and then, you can remember you ... cared for this guy once."

Her eyes filled with tears.

"I care for you now," she said.

"I am in love with you, Ophelia." I gave her the security she needed. It drained my own power more. "But now, I have to go."

"No," she grabbed me to her, pressed her head into my neck.

"I don't want to go, and I'll be back, a lot, I promise ... but I have to go now."

She stepped back and tilted her head on the side while she thought. I wanted to stay the night holding her in my arms and breathing her in.

"Can I ask you one question before you go?" she stared at me quizzically.

"Maybe, if it doesn't take a lot of detail to answer," I teased her and reached for her hand.

She smiled, the first time I had seen her smile for days and days.

"Are you all here?" she asked. "I mean, do you have a hole in your chest or a limb missing?"

I frowned, looked down at my feet, back at her and laughed. "Trust me, I'm all here. Where did you get that weird idea?"

She shrugged. "Research."

"You can do that first hand now," I told her. "But not right now, I have to go or I'm going to be too weak to ... another time." I kissed her again. "I will see you tomorrow, I promise." Then I turned and walked through her bedroom glass windows and disappeared into the night.

CHAPTER 17

HOLLY

"You're so much cheerier, today," I studied Ophelia. Well, she was. She looked different ... she had braided her hair, pulling it off her face and her eyes had a sparkle to them. All day she had been smiling, talking, joining in, a totally different Ophelia to the quiet person who started at the school almost a month ago now and only last week was like totally morose!

"Yeah, I'm feeling good," she shrugged.

"No, there's more to it than that," I teased her as we walked to English—our last class before lunch.

She rolled her eyes. "You're happy and I don't give you a hard time," Ophelia said.

"Yeah, but I'm half-glass-full happy. You're more like you're ..." I studied her, "boyfriend happy."

She laughed.

"C'mon spill it," I said. "Is it Chayse?"

"No!" she exclaimed, "not that there's anything wrong with Chayse of course, he's dreamy, but no, so not Chayse and it's not Adam either before you go there."

"Mm, who's left?" I asked.

"I do know more than two guys," she said, holding open the English classroom door for me.

"How? You've only been here for a minute," I reminded her.

Peggy was already there when we arrived and we took our seats next to her.

"I like your hair like that, Lia," Peggy said.

"Thanks, Peggy," Ophelia smiled. She dropped down in the middle desk and I took the other side and leaned over to Peggy.

"Has Harry ...?" I asked.

Peggy shook her head.

"Don't worry," I leaned over and patted her arm, "you're too good for my brother."

She blushed and smiled, looking away.

"So," I lowered my voice and returned my attention to Ophelia, "who is he? Does he go to this school or one of the others? Is he working?"

Ophelia looked around to ensure no-one was listening and said, "It's Jack. You saw him out of the window in art class, remember?"

"The cute guy with the long jacket?"

"That's him."

"Good for you," I nudged her. "You deserve to be happy."

She smiled. "Thanks, Holly. That's a really nice thing to say."

"Does he have a brother?" I asked.

Mm, so Ophelia was radiant with happiness, Peggy was wistful about Harry, me—well, I didn't have a date for the school dance, but it didn't matter ... I'd just go with the girls. It would be nice to be asked though.

It was literature debate afternoon. Mr Wall played English-lesson related games with us when he sensed the class was only half there—like just before lunch or for the last lesson of the day. He must have seen me daydreaming and sprung a question my way.

"So Holly, would you rather be Elizabeth Bennett from Jane Austen's *Pride and Prejudice* or Bridget Jones from Helen Fielding's *Bridget Jones's Diary*?" he asked.

"Trick question, Sir," I grinned. He wasn't going to get me on that one. "They're pretty much the same character just a different era."

He pushed his glasses further up his nose and wagged his finger at me. "Well done. I saw you daydreaming but you've pulled it off this time." I got some congratulatory grins from class members.

"So which one would you rather be?" he persisted.

I frowned thinking about it. "I think Bridget Jones. It must have been really frustrating being a woman in the time of *Pride and Prejudice*."

"Obeying men, what a great idea," Russell Sparke in the front row piped in. All the guys in the class cheered and Mr Wall encouraged the debate.

"Russell, you definitely are not a bright 'sparke' saying that in a class with more ladies than gents," Mr Wall teased him. "I hope your date for the dance isn't in this room, because you might be going alone now."

Russell grinned and shrugged. Mr Wall continued. "It is a truth universally acknowledged that Helen Fielding did not invent the entire plot of her novel *Bridget Jones's Diary*, she just brought *Pride and Prejudice* into the late 20th century and ..."

I zoned out again and looked out the window at the beautiful day outside. Eventually, the bell rang and we packed up. The four of us did an Elvis and left the building; Peggy and Harry fell behind to talk with Mr Wall. Outside, I saw Chayse coming from the other direction, he was staring at Ophelia but he couldn't get away from someone talking in his face.

"Lia, that's twice Chayse has tried to get your attention and you've dodged him," I nudged Ophelia as we lowered ourselves onto the grass underneath our favourite tree.

She bit her lower lip and looked in the direction of Chayse's group. Imogen and her girlfriends didn't hang with them anymore since the break-up, but somehow Tyler and Chayse's other friends had enough girls around them to still make it look like a harem.

"What if he wants to ask you out?" I asked Ophelia.

She laughed. "Yeah, that's likely. He's gone off beach bunnies and is now into pale, white ghosts." She smiled at the thought.

"It's an English beauty thing," I told her. "Like in *Pride and Prejudice*—all the girls are fair and feminine."

She snorted with laughter.

"Yeah, I'm sure they never laughed like that though," I said.

She gave me a shove. "Hey, Holly, look," she nodded towards the path. Harry and Peggy were walking towards us. "Do you think she cornered him?"

"They look kind of cute together," I studied them, "even with Harry's bad head."

"You're terrible," Ophelia said. "He's sweet and handsome in his own way."

They arrived and took up some grass. Peggy gave us both a sheepish grin and sat down beside Ophelia.

"Hello you two, what are you plotting?" Harry asked. "Nice hair, Lia."

"Thanks, Harry," Ophelia said brightly.

We talked about nothing for most of the lunch break and I bemoaned the fact that I didn't have a date for the dance yet.

"I'm taking Peggy," Harry piped up and Peggy blushed and nodded.

Ophelia and I tried to play it cool.

"Half your luck. Can't believe that Peggy agreed," I teased them both.

A shadow fell across us and we looked up to see Chayse standing there.

"Ah hi," he said. "Lia, any chance I could have a word?"

She gave me a panicked look.

"Sure," she began to rise and he extended his hand and helped her up. I watched them walk away.

"What's that about?" Harry asked.

"Beats me," I shrugged. "But I think he likes her and if Lia wants my advice, I think she should set him free immediately. The biggest mistake you can make in love is pining for someone who isn't interested ... unrequited love," I sighed.

"How would you know?" Harry asked.

"I read it in a book," I told him.

"I bet he asks her to the dance," Peggy said with a smile to Harry.

Great I'm going to be the gooseberry or was it a raspberry? Whatever!

JACK

She was so radiant and I couldn't take the smile off my face just watching her. She did something with her hair today, plaited, and it looked so sweet. I watched her in art class; I let her get just a glimpse of me and it was worth it for the look of happiness it brought to her face. Tonight I would kiss and hold her again. I would tell her what it means to me to be with her and what we had to do to be together, forever. But only if I think she's ready for that.

Then, I saw her walk away with the tall surfer. If my heart still beat, it would have stopped for the chill that ran through my veins at the sight of them together. She's mine now and I am not prepared to lose her. I'm not alive nor am I dead but with her, I'm reborn.

I walked beside them, beside Ophelia. I didn't show myself but I would step up if she needed me. Chayse was nervous, I could read him. He cleared his throat.

"I guess you've heard that Imogen and I have split," he said, pushing his hands into his pockets.

Ophelia nodded. "I'm sorry."

"That's okay. It was a long time coming. I tried to call it off at the end of school term last year, but she didn't want to break up, and over the Christmas holidays we sort of got back together again," he said. "Did you leave anyone behind in Brisbane?"

Ophelia shook her head "No. I've never had a real boyfriend."

The longing for her flooded me and I wanted to appear to her then and there. I could feel Chayse's desire for her rise. I want to be her first, her only and her last. I breathed her in.

They stopped at reaching the school boundary and Chayse turned face-on to Ophelia.

"I was just wondering if maybe you might like to go out, you know catch a movie this weekend?" he asked, "maybe go to the dance together?"

Ophelia's eyes widened in surprise and she giggled. Chayse looked embarrassed then a bit angry.

"Sorry," she said. "It's just that you could have any girl in this school, and I am so, well not your type."

Chayse shrugged. "How do you know? We don't really know each other that well and anyway, they say opposites attract."

She touched his arm and I moved in quickly—I couldn't help myself, I rushed at her. Ophelia felt me; she rubbed her arm where goose bumps appeared and looked around for me. Ever so slightly she shook her head, telling me not to be concerned.

"Thank you, Chayse. I'm super flattered, really, who wouldn't be?" she told him. "But I've met someone."

I was in heaven.

"Really?" Chayse asked.

Ophelia rolled her eyes. "You're as bad as Adam," she said. Chayse bristled at the comparison. "Is it so hard to believe that someone might ask me out?"

"No I didn't mean that. It's just that you haven't been here that long ... it's not Adam is it?"

"What if it was?" Ophelia asked. I could read she was getting impatient with their feud.

Chayse's jaw tightened and he shrugged. "He's not good enough for you."

Now I knew Ophelia was angry, I could feel her heart rate quicken and I wasn't all that happy that she was defending one and talking to the other. Get lost surfer guy.

She drew a deep breath and forced herself to smile. "Adam's like a brother to me."

"That's good," Chayse grinned.

"And," she continued, "he's been really good to me."

Chayse nodded. "Okay, I might have overstepped."

"But you've been really kind to me too, Chayse, thank you. You've made being the new kid just a bit easier," she gave him a smile that would melt any heart, "and thank you for asking me."

He reddened. "So who's this guy?"

"You don't know him. He's new to the area too, I guess it's what we have in common," she said. Her eyes softened as she spoke of me.

The bell for the last few classes of the day rang, signalling lunch was over. As soon as it was nightfall, and she could get away, I would have her all to myself.

CHAPTER 18

OPHELIA

I wasn't going straight home after school, I had some research to do. I was going to the cemetery to find Jack's grave. I don't know if my actions would cheese Jack off, but I didn't want to ask him and risk driving him away. I wanted to find the grave by myself, first. I checked out the bus route and it meant changing buses twice—way too hard. I would have to fork out for a taxi, but given I had a weekly allowance from my parent's life insurance and I had spent zilch since arriving, it was no big deal.

After the last class, I told my tribe I had a doctor's appointment—yeah no one wants to know anything more about that—and I waited for the taxi I had booked on my phone between my last two classes. When it arrived around the corner from the school, I slipped into the back seat, gave the driver the address and was there in less than ten minutes. If I had a bike, I could have hiked it there easily. I thanked the driver, paid him and he said he was sorry for my loss. Me too.

I stood at the entrance gate. It was huge and kind of beautiful—the cemetery even had water views. I grabbed my phone, flipped to my notes and checked the aisle and plot number. It was in the Church of England section, compartment twenty-eight, grave seventeen. Can't be too hard, I thought and looked around for the signs. I wandered for a while amongst the graves, heading towards the oldest part of the Church of England section where Jack lay. Now that sounded weird.

In the distance I saw an elderly lady cleaning up a grave, I averted my eyes to give her privacy. I know what it is like to have everyone gawking at you when you want to be alone to deal with your grief or even just to chat with your family—dead or alive. Wow, I'm truly living in both worlds at the moment!

I found the correct row, now I just needed to find the grave. I checked the number again and wandered along. I found the location but there was no headstone. I looked again, it was an unmarked grave. Why? Why didn't he have a headstone with his name on it and the dates of his birth and death—Jack Denham, tragically taken at sea, 1888-1905, or something like that? It's like he never existed. I knelt in the area of the unmarked grave and just looked at it. It was so weird to be looking at the grave of the guy that I had fallen for in a major way—a dead guy that I would be seeing tonight. I shivered at the thought.

"Here is where you lie, Jack," I whispered and closed my eyes. I couldn't feel him, he wasn't here. He stayed around the water, maybe because that's where he loved to be and that's where his life ended.

My phone pinged with a text message and I jumped with fright. Scaredy cat ... but it was so quiet at the cemetery that every noise made me jump. I looked at the text and it was from Adam asking me to wait for him to walk the dogs. I texted back I was still in Warrnambool and he rang.

"So am I," he said cutting to the chase. "I'm just leaving work now, want a lift?"

"Yes please!" I brightened. That saved waiting for the next bus or forking out way too much for a taxi. "I'm at the cemetery."

ADAM

This kid is too bizarre—okay maybe Ophelia is not a kid anymore, she is sixteen and probably more mature than most having lost her folks, but the cemetery? Really? I wonder if I should let Sebastian know. Who does she even know to visit or what exactly is she planning that involves hanging around the cemetery? I realised I was driving too fast and slowed down—she wasn't in danger that I knew of, just hanging around the cemetery!

From what I could tell, Ophelia spent half of the time pretending everything was great—as though having your mother and father die on the same day, changing States, changing schools, changing lives, was all in her control—and the rest of her time hiding in her bedroom. I swear I've heard her talking to herself up there or talking to someone. She's different too—every other teen has headphones or earphones stuck in their ears and are totally self-absorbed but not Lia. She claims to not want the noise filling her head; she wants to have think time. She's going to blow up; her head will scatter everywhere, seriously.

As I approached the entrance gates to the cemetery I saw her waiting near the bricked wall. She smiled, grabbed her bag and raced over to the car.

"Hey Adam, thanks for the lift, brilliant," she said jumping into my four-wheel drive which I didn't really need for an apprentice boat builder role but it was great for fitting the surfboard, bike and mates in. Vanessa didn't like it though—not sophisticated enough for her— she wanted me to get a sports car.

So here was Ophelia; all cheery and sweet.

"My pleasure. I might be a bit dirty, sorry," I said noticing the grease on my legs.

"You are!" she wrinkled her nose in mock disgust and smiled.

"You okay?" I asked.

"Yes, thanks. How are you?" she looked at me.

I hate how she deflected, damn but she was good at it.

"I'm good," I said slowly and deliberately, "but I'm not hanging around the cemetery." We began the twenty minute drive home. "Ophelia?"

She looked over at me. "Yes, Adam?"

I grinned at her formality. "Can I ask what exactly you were doing at the cemetery?"

She exhaled and looked away, watching the landscape from her passenger side window. I felt her stiffen beside me. I knew it was only a matter of time until she broke down, no one could keep up that front.

"Lia?" I prodded. The very core of me wanted to pull the car over and hold her and tell her everything would be alright eventually, but I didn't know her well enough to do that yet and she might get out of the car and run.

She turned to look at me, bit her lip and looked truly upset. I almost wish I hadn't said anything now.

"Adam, promise you won't tell anyone?" she started.

I nodded. "I told you that you could trust me." I manoeuvred the car through a roundabout and we were on the road home to Port Fairy.

She didn't speak for a moment. "Lia?"

"I was ..."

"Yes," I gently nudged her along.

"I was doing my assignment!" she grinned and then laughed out loud.

I gave her a wry look and shook my head.

"Adam, lighten up. What do you think I'm doing at the cemetery, buying a plot? Visiting someone else's parents?"

"Fine. So sorry for being concerned," I said. I wasn't really cranky, I just wanted her to feel bad for making me feel like an idiot.

"Thank you for caring," she leaned over and kissed me on the cheek.

My eyes narrowed. "You'll keep Ophelia Montague. One day, you may just need me and I won't be there because you've cried wolf too many times."

"Won't you be there?" she looked at me with her head on the side.

"Yeah, I probably will," I sighed.

OPHELIA

One of my pet hates, a major pet hate, is that when you're going through some tough stuff everyone is looking at you all the time, watching you, waiting for you to lose it or have a major breakdown. I can't bear the sympathetic looks, I can't stand the supportive glances. Get over it everyone! Right, I feel better now. I know Adam meant well, he's a sweetie but honestly, what did he think I was doing at the cemetery? Getting a dose of morbid because my stock was running low?

He interrupted my thoughts as we sat in his car on the way home.

"I could have taken you to the cemetery on the weekend," he said, "save you getting stranded. How did you get there?"

"Taxi," I said.

"How were you going to get home?" he asked.

"The bus. I just had to get to the nearest stop for the Port Fairy route. Besides I'm sure you've got better things to do on the weekend than go to the cemetery with me, and I figured I had already used up my favours," I smiled at him. He looked kind of ruggard and handsome in his work gear, Vanessa's loss. I wondered what she was like, Holly would know.

"I enjoy it," he said, "I don't get to do the tourist and history thing very often and to be honest, even though she drives me nuts, I do miss my little sister and her constant chauffeuring demands to ballet, netball, softball, the beach, the best friend's house ..."

We arrived and Adam steered the car up the long driveway to our house. Our house. It looked surprised as always. Sitting up in the attic windows lying in the warm sun were Argo and Agnes. I saw them recognise Adam's car and its sound, stand up and begin the bolt downstairs. Adam pulled into the car port and cut the ignition.

"Thank you, bro," I teased him. "I really appreciate it!"

"Too easy. Next time, text me," he said. "Most days I come through Warrnambool unless I'm off somewhere on a job."

We headed in for dog licks and tail wagging, and we checked in on Uncle Seb—he worked at home on Mondays.

"We're going for a walk, we'll take the dogs. Can you come, Uncle Seb?" I asked.

"Afraid not, but have fun and thanks for taking the furry kids, otherwise I'd have no choice, they'd bully me to the beach. I'll take them in the morning."

"I love taking them," I told him with a wave at the door. I raced upstairs to change. I really wanted to go alone to see if Jack appeared but I would have to be content to wait until tonight now. When I went back down, Adam was in his board shorts and T-shirt, with an open hoodie on.

"I'm going in for a quick swim too," he grabbed his towel. "You coming in?"

I rolled my eyes. "You know at home, we can always pick the people from across the border—want to know how?"

He gave me a wry look. "Tell me."

"They're the only ones in the water in winter because they think it's our summer!" I teased.

He laughed. "So too cold for you then is it you big girl?"

"Yeah, I'm a big girl," I agreed. "C'mon Argo and Agnes, you've got more sense," I said avoiding the flick of Adam's towel as we headed out.

All four of us couldn't wait to get on the beach for different reasons. Maybe Jack would appear while Adam was in swimming, or maybe he would save his strength for later, but I knew he would be beside me in some form.

We crossed the road and I felt the new but now familiar calmness that seeing the ocean and feeling the sand between my toes brought on. Argo and Agnes circled us, running down to the water's edge and back to us over and over. It felt so good. I looked around, feeling like I was really opening my eyes and seeing the day for the first time today. How different this was to my life only a few months ago.

"Sure you don't want to change your mind?" Adam asked.

"Brrr," I said.

"Right then," he gave me his towel to hold. "I'll catch you up." He pulled off his hoodie and slipped off his T-shirt over his head, I reached out for it as well. He turned and ran down to the water's edge, all tanned and taut. The scenery was great, but he was insane—it was super chilly.

I started walking and greeted an older man as he passed me. I had met him and his large black Labrador, Frodo, before. Argo, Agnes and Frodo greeted each other like long lost friends. I kept walking in the lighthouse direction and the dogs followed. There were no surfers and I was relieved that I didn't have to see Chayse or his pack. Then I felt him; the cool touch of Jack beside me and I smiled. He whispered my name but I still couldn't see him.

"Jack," I said softly. I didn't want to be the weird girl talking to herself on the beach ... again. "I'll be back later tonight after I finish my homework and once Uncle Seb turns in," I said, closing my eyes for a moment and feeling his soft touch and the trace of coolness on my face. "I can't wait to see you," I opened my eyes and blinked away the tears. I could have sworn he just kissed me, his cold lips pressed against mine. I know he could appear, but I'm glad he didn't—it built up my desire to see him and meant he would be stronger with me tonight.

CHAPTER 19

OPHELIA

I couldn't find him when I arrived on the beach; it was dark, a cloudy night and maybe that was a good thing so we could hide. As I walked towards our rock, I suddenly felt him and then he was there, holding my hand and walking beside me.

I'm sure my eyes and face lit with excitement, giving me away. So much for acting cool, I was gone.

"You did that as though we've been walking along together for ages," I looked at my hand in his.

"We have," he said, his dimples showing as he teased me. "I've been beside you most of the day. I missed you, even when I was beside you. Can't say I was too happy with you being so close to the surfer and Adam." He stopped, faced me, and pulled me in for a deep kiss.

I couldn't breathe, I didn't want to breathe, I just wanted this to last.

When he pulled away, he placed a soft kiss on my forehead and raised my chin so we looked into each other's eyes.

I was teary again. Good grief. I tried to look away but he wouldn't let me and he cupped my face in his hands.

"I love you Ophelia Montague."

I did cry now and smile. "I love you Jack Denham," I said back to him.

"You have no idea how long I've waited for you," he said. "Stop crying or I'll be worried I've upset you."

"You have," I declared. "You've shown me something that I now can't be without and nothing will ever match up to. If anything should happen to you Jack, to separate us ..."

"Shh," he said and kissed me to stop me from talking. He kissed my top lip and drank in the salty tear that had rolled there.

Jack pulled me closer and he might have been a ghost, but I could feel his body pressing against me. "We don't have to be apart ever," he whispered as he held me tight, his hand in my hair and the other pressing into my back. "Ever."

I didn't want to stop holding each other but I had to breathe. He took my hand again and we began our walk to the rock.

"I want to hear your story; I want you to tell me every detail about you and your life," I said.

"My short life and long after life," he joked. The tide was out; it was dry and safe. This time he didn't lead me up our rock by the hand, instead he scooped me up and I wrapped my arms around his neck, watching his face as he so easily carried me to the top and placed me down. We lowered ourselves to the rock and he sat around me, his arm and legs entwining me in the darkness, as I sat back against his chest. It felt so perfect—like no-one or nothing else existed in the world except us two.

"Can you feel that?" I asked. "That we are the only two people in the world."

"We are," he agreed.

I thought about my past crushes; it was nothing like this. Jack read me.

"People will say we feel this intensity because we're young or because it is your first love and my first real love, but it is not true—it is not always like this," he told me.

137

"I know," I said. "I've seen my parents and relatives and friends' relationships. I've read about love in books and seen it in movies. I've had crushes; I know a love like this is not what everyone gets."

He rubbed his cheek against mine as we looked out to sea. I melted into him and then he pulled away, inhaling sharply. He closed his eyes. "Woah, you drain me my love," he tried to regain control.

"I'm sorry," I turned to him.

"I'm not," he answered.

"I thought love was supposed to make you stronger," I said.

Jack smiled and opened his eyes; they were as dark as the ocean.

"Did you read that in your 'How to identify a ghost' manual?" he teased.

I nodded and grinned.

He laughed and squeezed me tightly. We sat enjoying being totally absorbed in each other.

"Tell me your story, Jack," I prompted him. I turned side-on so I could watch him.

He looked out to the ocean and began.

JACK

"I was born in Melbourne in 1888," I waited for her reaction.

"You're way too old for me," she said with a straight face.

"You're right, I'll go," I teased and she grabbed onto me quickly and kissed me. She pulled away and I watched as she opened her eyes, she had a dreamy look. "Don't even joke about that," she warned me.

"This story is going to take a long time if you keep distracting me," I scolded her.

She bit her lip and nodded. "Right, I won't touch you again until you finish it."

"Sure you won't," I teased. I didn't want her watching me; it's a hard story for me to tell. I nudged her around so we both looked out to sea and wrapped my arms around her. She leaned back into me. I would have to choose my words carefully, she was still raw from losing her own parents and I didn't want her to associate me with death.

Now I could tell the story without watching her emotions rise or Lia studying mine; that would be easier for me—I didn't go back in the past much and think about my family or that night. I took a deep breath of salt air and recalled my past.

〜

OPHELIA

Jack looked pale—I knew I was draining him, I think that's why he didn't want me looking at him. I don't mean to drain him, I don't know how not too, we just have this intensity between us.

I wanted to watch his face as he told me the story, but I nestled next to his cheek, where I could glance up at him and listen to his voice in my ear. Straight ahead the moon was struggling to break free from the dark clouds. The ocean looked black; I didn't want to think what was out there. He cleared his throat interrupting my fears and started his story.

"I'm an only child, that is, I was an only child. We didn't have a lot and since the day I could walk and talk, I wanted to go to sea. I found work on a ship as a ship's boy—it's usually where a young sailor starts out. Heard of it?" he asked.

I shook my head. "What did you do?"

"Whatever everyone else didn't want to do," he said with a laugh. "Pretty much whatever the captain wanted me to do or needed me to do. The captain said I had potential—I liked him, and I was going to work my way up. It was a good role to start in because you did everything; you got to know how to work sails, lines and ropes in all sorts of weather and I'd stand watch or act as helmsman sometimes. The best part was just being free. I loved being out on the ocean."

"I know you have saltwater in your veins," I told him.

He smiled "I do in more ways than one."

The thought freaked me out a little and he read me.

"Sorry," his jaw set. "That was stupid of me. Ophelia, you're not going to like everything I tell you and maybe you'll be repulsed by what I am when I finish."

"No," I sat upright and turned. I touched his face. "I won't be. I'm just ... I'm frightened by the ocean, not by you."

He nodded. From the set of his lips, I was not sure I convinced him, but he smiled, even if his eyes didn't and turned me again to fall back into him.

"Continue," I ordered.

"Yes, Ma'am," he saluted and looked so gorgeous, I just wanted the night to go on forever. I glanced at my watch. It was just after midnight ... hours yet until sunrise, if I could just slow them down.

"The crew, we all got on; it was a mixed crew from different ports," Jack described his crewmates. "The Captain was from Timaru in New Zealand and we met his wife when we were docked. She didn't like him being away as much, but he always said he had a wife and a mistress and at least his mistress was the sea," Jack said, with a smile. "Most of the crew were single, it was easier if you wanted to live a sailor's life," Jack said. "Leonard the second mate was from Auckland, Able Seaman Oscar was another Kiwi," Jack said. "Able Seaman John was from Tassie, Richard was from Sydney. They all survived."

He stopped a moment and I glanced at him to read his face. It wasn't anger or jealousy; I couldn't tell. A few seconds passed and he continued.

"The rest of us didn't make it—Colson the first mate was from

Auckland. He was like a father to me and he had a wife and four kids; Charles the cook was also from Auckland, a single man; Gustave, another Kiwi sailor was single and Robert was from here, well, North Melbourne. He left behind a widow and family. Pierre was from France, he was your friend Chayse's ancestor and he was married with sons, and then my mate, Larry, an ordinary seaman was a year older than me and from Melbourne too."

"And you," I whispered, "my able seaman."

He grinned and pressed his face into my hair. I felt the coldness coming from his body at the memory of what was to come.

"You don't have to tell me if it is too hard," I said.

"You have to know," he said. "Am I chilling you too much?"

"No, I'm good," I assured him. "Tell me about the last day." I inhaled knowing it would be harrowing.

"To be honest, it was so fast and so slow it's hard to explain. Everything happened so quickly but yet I see some of it in slow motion. Weird?"

"No, I get that," I assured him. "At Mum and Dad's funeral, I felt like I was out of my body, watching it all below in slow motion. Yet the days before and after are a blur, I can't remember anything."

"Grief," he said. "Funny thing. But on a cheerier note, you have to know, I was happy. I was where I wanted to be. But I had already had a scare, me and Larry—that's Larry Watson; he was a few years older than me—we were both wrecked on the Kaipara bar in a ship called the Emerald in August last, but all onboard survived that one. It was foggy weather but we were lucky that time, we got ashore in boats and not long after the vessel went to pieces."[1]

"And you got back on another ship after that?" I exclaimed. "Nothing would get me on another ship ever!"

Jack grinned. "You should hear Eva's story, Eva Carmichael. She was on a ship called the Loch Ard which sank nearby, just off the shipwreck coast. Eva and one other man were the only survivors from a whole ship. Then she got on another ship and returned to Ireland. Now that was tempting fate."

"You're both crazy," I shook my head, surprised at the pang of jealousy I felt with Jack mentioning another female who was long dead.

"Yeah she was cute," he read me, and seeing my eyes widened, he laughed heartily. I gave him a push and he grabbed me closer.

"Ophelia, you're too much," he laughed.

"Too much what?" I asked indignantly.

"Too much beauty, heart, brains and too much for me!" he sighed.

I smiled and looked out to sea so that he wouldn't see the colour rising from my neck.

Jack smiled and continued. "Anyway, Larry and I got work on the La Bella and after that, Larry was going back to Auckland, and I was going to stay in Melbourne for a while. The La Bella was only about six-years-old and in great condition. Once the timber was loaded, we sailed. "I wasn't on the watch that night but I heard the bells and it was ten o'clock when the trouble began. It was a really misty night and we were already overdue with the timber load by a couple of days. As we got closer to land, the sea was so heavy that it was breaking over the hull. I didn't think for a minute I'd be in danger again so soon, but it wasn't looking good. She was rolling heavily and it looked like the La Bella was going to go to pieces." He took a deep breath.

Ghosts do breath.

"I can't explain what it was like; loud, dark, freezing," Jack continued. "We saw a whaleboat heading towards us coming to help. Sometimes you could just hear shouts from them or from us, and I could see people on shore watching us. God, I wanted to be one of them."

My breathing quickened as he told the story. I stole a glance at Jack, his face was stony.

He continued[2]: "the ship was like a toy ... honestly, Ophelia, I tried to hold on; I couldn't swim. I saw the other men trying to do the same but no one could get near us to help and the waves, it didn't stop. Our ship, she kept rolling and righting herself and rolling again. We were wet and chilled to the bone. I couldn't feel anything and it went on for hours and hours with no relief.

"I saw the lifeboats a few times but they couldn't get close enough. They even tried throwing ropes but no luck. I don't know what time it was or how many hours had passed. Some of the crew lashed themselves to the woodwork so they wouldn't get swept off the ship. We were all gesturing for help but no-one could help us."

I had tears rolling down my face and Jack stopped and leaned in close to me.

"Don't cry Ophelia, it's over now. You shouldn't fear death," he said.

"But you had such an agonising death," I wiped my eyes with my sleeve.

"Yeah, you can only die once though," he said matter-of-factly. "It can't hurt me ever again. I won't say anymore tonight."

"You must," I insisted. "I'm alright, really, please don't leave me hanging."

Jack studied me, nodded and continued.

"I was so exhausted and frozen that I couldn't feel my arms or legs anymore. I knew I was hanging on because I could see my hands clinging to the rope, but I couldn't feel them. I saw it play out in front of me but I was helpless—I didn't know what time it was but I learnt later that it was two o'clock when my friend Larry, who survived the last shipwreck with me, and our cook Charles were both washed away. They were strapped to the fore rigging but were unconscious from exposure when it happened. I guess that was a blessing.

"I would have been washed overboard and drowned too except that John—seaman Noake—kept me alive. He was holding me and himself on to the ship with both of his arms wrapped around me. Then, the anchor which weighed a ton and a half was wrenched away. That should give you an indication of how wild it was. It just wouldn't stop though, wouldn't stop!"

Jack's voice rose and I reached up for him and kissed him on the lips. I felt his body relax into me.

"I'm okay," he sighed pulling away. "I have to tell you ... let me finish so we can never speak of it again."

I nodded and watched him with concern.

"Five more hours we held on ... five more wretched hours. The sun began to rise and I have since been told it was seven o'clock, just before the last man was rescued—I felt the waves take me. A heavy sea lifted me away and John had done his best but I was taken. I'm so pleased he survived, he's a hero."

I understood now what Jack meant about every man helping each other and being heroic in their efforts and why Chayse wanted some sort of acknowledgement for the loss of lives. Tears streamed down my face and I couldn't look at Jack.

"Obviously I was not around to see what happened to my sea mates, maybe that was a blessing, but I have found out since, I've heard the tales," he said.

"Tell me," I encouraged him to finish.

Jack continued. "When the ship began to sink, two of the crew jumped overboard in the direction of the lifeboat—it was about one hundred yards away, I think that is about ninety metres in your modern speak—and they were trying to swim or stay afloat. That's when William Ferrier rowed towards them right into the huge waves and grabbed two of them—one was our Captain who refused to leave the ship until the last.

"William knew how to row that dinghy; he spun it around before the next roller hit and managed to get the men to shore. A miracle really," Jack shook his head.

"Where was the other lifeboat?" I asked.

"Still out there. It picked up one of the swimmers and William went back out again. Two men could be seen clinging to the ship as it went under. The lifeboat got closer and the rescuers were yelling for the men to jump, but I don't know whether they were too frozen or too scared, but they stood like statues. Finally, one of them jumped and swam about eight yards—um," Jack did the calculation in his head—"just over seventy metres and got pulled into the lifeboat."

I cheered and realised I had been holding my breath. Jack laughed.

"You are a wonderful storyteller, you should let me get your version down," I told him.

"And how would you tell people you got it?" he teased.

"Ah yeah, good point. I'd think of something."

"I think you'll find it's all out there already—lots of records in the old newspapers."

"If it happened today, there would be a book, a movie, a website, you name it," I told him. "Keep going please Jack," I said, with a glance to my watch. It was nearing two a.m. and the time had flown as we filled it with shared silence, holding each other and kisses. I wasn't a bit tired, even though I had school in six hours.

Jack lay back on the rock and I lay beside him. He balled his coat up and put it under our heads. We looked up at the sky which was threatening rain now.

"Where was I?" Jack thought. "Oh yeah, so now only one sailor remained to be rescued. Five of us were gone to the sea and seven would be saved. Again, it was William who saved the day. He sculled to the stern of the vessel which was almost level with the water's edge now and he picked up our last man. Everyone was cheering from the shore."

"I can see why Adam's family line is revered," I said.

"And that's my story. I drowned in Lady Bay. But here I am. And here you are." He sighed and sat up. I joined him. "I can't speak any more tonight," he said. I touched his very pale skin. "Soon, let's talk of us and our future."

Jack lowered his head, placing his forehead on mine and closed his eyes.

We stayed that way for a short while and then Jack pulled away.

"Just know that I want you and I have waited for a long time for you. Let me see you home, while I still have the strength."

CHAPTER 20

OPHELIA

*H*olly nudged me awake. I looked around, wiped the drool from the corner of my mouth and prayed that no-one else in my economics class noticed. It was nearing the lunch break and I was just going to make it; I had only fallen asleep twice today.

"Thanks," I whispered to her and pretended to keep reading, which we were supposed to be doing—the whole chapter on price formation, kill me now. The truth was I was cranky tired and ecstatically happy. I never ever thought after Mum and Dad died that I could be this happy ... in fact I didn't know you could be so happy in love at all. Jack was all I could think of pretty much every minute of the waking day and a bit in my dreams, but I hadn't had much sleep of late. Between spending all night with him and spending all night awake thinking of him, I knew it couldn't go on like this for much longer. I would have to balance it somehow ... but I didn't want to at the moment, I just wanted to see him as much as I could. Then I worried was I seeing him too much, would we burn out? Could we burn out? More importantly, could I drain him to the point that he couldn't appear to me? Where was his power going? Not to me; I wasn't feeling stronger. My thoughts were interrupted by the ringing of the bell. I looked to Holly with relief and we stuffed our books in our bags.

Mr Tineham called out something about finishing that chapter for homework, we all groaned as expected and I followed Holly out of the classroom. We waited for Peggy and Harry to catch-up.

"I know what you're thinking," Peggy said hurrying along beside us as we headed outdoors. Holly frowned, Harry shook his head and I had learnt just to play along.

Peggy didn't wait for a response. "It's three days until the dance and we haven't talked about dresses."

"You're right," I said, "that's what we should be thinking," I agreed.

"That's because you're the only one with a date," Holly nudged Peggy.

"But why are you thinking that, Peggy?" I teased her, "that's not like you."

She reddened. "I know but now that I have a date, I need something to wear."

Harry covered his ears. "Don't talk dresses in front of me; you are all supposed to surprise me with your beauty on the night." He looked in Holly's direction. "Well just do your best."

"Shut up," she smirked at him.

We headed towards our tree and saw a group of younger students already there.

"Got to move these kids along," Harry said, "that's our tree."

Holly rolled her eyes. "We don't technically own it," she reminded him.

"Hey you guys," Harry said as we approached, "the principal's on his way here and he's looking for your year group to form a line for emu parade. I'd go undercover."

The four students jumped up, grabbed their bags, thanked Harry and bolted.

"Emu parade?" I asked, taking the patch of grass where one of them had just vacated.

"You know, you all get in a line, peck at the ground and pick up papers," Harry said. "What did they teach you at your other school?"

I punched his arm. "Clearly nothing important."

Holly leaned back against the tree, and rolling up my jumper I placed it in her lap and lay back for a nap.

"You've fallen asleep twice today already," she said. "Once in your economic textbook ..."

"That put us all to sleep," Harry said pulling a sandwich out of his lunchbox and offering one around. We all declined.

"And," Holly continued, "you nearly burnt your eyebrows snoozing near that Bunsen burner in biology. What's going on? Are you spending every night with your new boyfriend?"

Peggy's eyes widened with interest and Harry sparked up.

"New guy huh? Anyone we know?" he asked with a mouthful of ham and tomato sandwich. "Why does Mum insist on putting tomato on our lunch?" He waved the sandwich towards Holly. "Soggy."

I ignored the sandwich talk and told Harry who the new guy was. "Jack," I mumbled his name, while I was pleasantly dozing off. I loved saying his name.

HOLLY

I absent-mindedly stroked Ophelia's long, dark hair as she lay in my lap—my mum does that, so relaxing.

"Is Jack from this school?" Peggy asked.

"Nope," Ophelia said with a yawn.

"Shame he can't come to the dance then," Peggy said.

"That's okay," Ophelia said.

"Lia can be my date. You are coming aren't you?" I prodded her awake.

She brushed me away with annoyance. "Yeah, this Friday night, wouldn't miss it for anything. We'll go together," she agreed, "but I'll let you off the hook if you get a better offer before then."

I scoffed. "Three days away, not likely. We could go dress shopping after school," Holly suggested. "I've only got about fifty dollars saved so it will have to be the direct factory outlet area."

"Sounds great, I've got about the same and Dad's credit card," Peggy brightened. "I'll text Mum. Can you come, Lia?"

"Sure. I'll see if Adam can pick us up on his way through after work, if we'll be done by about five," Ophelia offered.

"For a lift home with Adam, I could be finished before I start," I told her.

Harry shook his head. "Well don't worry about me, I'll catch the bus as usual and see you at home."

"Sure, whatever." I told my twin.

Peggy gave my loser brother a winning smile.

"What's your favourite colour?" she asked him.

"Irrelevant," I reminded Peggy. "What's important is what colour looks best on you so that you look fantastic."

"Fetching," Ophelia mumbled. "Jack says fetching."

"Wow, he's stuck in a time warp," Harry smirked. "Working from an early Oxford dictionary is he?"

"I think it's charming," I reprimanded Harry.

"Me too," Ophelia smiled, still lying with her eyes closed.

She really was gone for this guy.

OPHELIA

"You're a brave man, Adam," Uncle Seb said as he passed Adam the salt and pepper. We sat around the dining table, with Argo and

Agnes nearby. They had finished their dinner and lay where they were handy for leftovers.

"Really, Uncle Seb," I teased, "some might say lucky!"

"True," Adam agreed. "Getting to drive home two beautiful young women flushed with shopping success talking boys all the way home ... yep, make my day."

"Thanks for picking Holly and me up," I added.

"That's a pleasure, I was coming through anyway. I would have dropped Peggy home in Warrnambool too and saved her mum coming out."

"Her mum is pretty strict," I told him. "I don't think she would have let Peggy in the car with anyone that she hadn't run a police check on."

"Any luck with the shopping?" Uncle Seb asked.

"Peggy and Holly both got new dresses," Adam answered for me with a grin. "I heard about it all the way home. A lovely shade of red for Peggy which goes with her exotic Asian features, dark hair and brown eyes, and a jade coloured dress for Holly to bring out her green eyes, apparently."

Uncle Seb and I both laughed.

"You're freaking me out," I told Adam.

"Didn't you get anything Lia, do you need some cash?" Uncle Seb looked concerned.

I shook my head and finished my mouthful of Mrs Duck's sausage, eggplant and tomato casserole before answering. "Thanks Uncle Seb, but I've got plenty of allowance left. No one here has seen my wardrobe, so all my clothes are new here. I've got a few dresses I can wear on Friday night."

"Who are you going with?" Adam asked.

"Holly."

"Oh, well that's nice," Uncle Seb said. I noticed he tried to look indifferent.

"We're not gay," I assured him, "although if I was, Holly would probably be my type," I mused on this and noticed Adam gave me a strange look. "But no, we're both just dateless."

"Shame I can't help you out and take you, but I assume it's still present students only?" Adam asked.

"Eew," I said, "how uncool ... my 'brother' has to take me to the dance because no one else will."

He rolled his eyes, grinned and looked at Uncle Seb.

"Well that's gratitude for you."

I laughed. "I chose to go alone because ..." I hesitated, then plunged in, "Chayse asked me but I said no, because I do like someone, but he doesn't go to our school."

I dropped two bombs on Adam there and waited for his response. I knew Uncle Seb would be pleased. Luckily Adam was eating at the time and systematically adding to a pile of eggplant on the side of his plate which he had tried to extract from the casserole. Uncle Seb stepped in.

"That was nice of Chayse. So he's broken up with that girl he's always on the beach with."

"Imogen, yes, for the second time in a matter of months," I said. Good grief, I was sounding like the school gossip.

"Keep up, Seb," Adam ribbed him which got us all laughing. "Well, I'm glad you didn't go with Chayse."

"I'm sure you are," I responded putting my knife and fork down.

"So who's this new guy?" Adam continued, his blue eyes interrogating me.

"No one you need to worry about thanks, Dad," I said.

Uncle Seb laughed and Adam grinned, as he pushed a dark strand of his hair back out of his eyes. "Don't make Seb and I resort to spying on you, Ophelia," he used my full name to indicate trouble.

"Just try it," I warned.

"Ah yes," Uncle Seb stepped in, "I'm not very good at this guardian thing." He wiped his mouth with a napkin and rising, took my plate and his and headed to the sink. "I'm probably supposed to ask more questions about the new boyfriend."

"It's all good," I assured them both. "His name is Jack, he's a gentleman."

"Where does he work and live?" Adam asked.

"Warrnambool and Warrnambool in that order," I embellished the truth a little.

"How old is he?" Adam asked.

"A year older than me and a year younger than you."

"What does he do for work?" Adam continued.

I frowned at him. "If Uncle Seb trusts me, then you can too. Otherwise, expect the worst—your next girlfriend will get a grilling."

He rose and taking his plate, joined Uncle Seb at the sink. I got up and made a fresh pot of tea for the three of us.

"Well I can't tell you how pleased I am, Lia," Uncle Seb said. "So happy you've settled in so well with good friends and now a boyfriend. I couldn't have asked for more."

"Thanks Uncle Seb," I kissed his cheek as his hands remained immersed in soapy dishwasher. He blushed and cleared his throat. "Now speaking of trust … I'm away from Monday for a week at a conference in Adelaide. I'm delivering a paper on the 'Vital history of shipbuilding and repair in Victoria' and I have a little research I want to do while I'm in the area. I'll be back Saturday afternoon. Mrs Ducks will be here to cook and clean as usual during the week but you'll be fending for yourselves for Friday night dinner. Will you both be okay and can you look after my precious kids?" he said, with a look to Argo and Agnes.

"Sure," Adam said. "We'll just carry on as usual."

"I'll walk Argo and Agnes every day," I said with a glance to the two dogs who wagged their tails on hearing their names.

"And I'll feed them," Adam added. "Lia can rustle up a meal Friday night," he said teasing me. He read my expression well. "Okay, well there's always cereal."

Uncle Seb looked upwards and the house moaned lightly. He nodded as though sharing a silent thought with the house. "Goodo, well that works out well then."

CHAPTER 21

OPHELIA

When I went up to my room after dinner to get my textbooks, I felt Jack before I saw him—the air turned cold around me. I wheeled around and there he was—so gorgeous.

I'm sure he could hear my heartbeat going a thousand beats a minute—it was embarrassing that it was obvious I was completely taken by him.

He held a finger to my lips and I didn't speak a word.

"Close your eyes," he said softly.

I did as he told me and then he seemed to be all around me; I was surrounded by his kisses, embrace, touch, electricity and cool space enveloping me. It was the most surreal feeling ever like being caught up in a heady whirlwind of love and angst and I began to go weak at the knees. He supported me before I slid to the ground, and pressed me against the wall.

I opened my eyes and exhaled. I could only just see him; my eyes were glazed like I was love drunk.

"How did you do that?" I whispered.

Jack grinned his boyish grin and it only made matters worse.

"I'm not seeing you tonight," he said.

"No," I began to protest. "I've waited all day."

He kissed me to silence me. Then kissed me more frantically before pushing away. We were both breathless.

"Right," he said, "Got to go. You need sleep tonight. We have plenty of time Ophelia, all the time in the world. Tonight you sleep."

I felt devastated.

"You can call me Lia," I sulked.

He shook his head. "Never. Ophelia is a great beauty, you own that name. *Hamlet* loved her more than 'forty thousand' brothers could. He was mad with lovesickness for her."

I smiled at him, looking into his beautiful face and dark, ocean blue eyes. I knew the story well, not only because I was named Ophelia but I copped Hamlet in year ten.

"You've been doing your research," I said, guessing he would never have studied *Hamlet* in his schooling.

"Indeed I have," he said. "Ophelia is goodness, sweetness and light. Naive but capable of great love, even when treated unkindly," he said, interpreting Shakespeare's Ophelia, not me.

"That's not me," I said. "I've had my eyes opened a lot in the last six months ..."

"It's you more than you know," Jack said.

"Then you know Ophelia drowned," I whispered the words, not wanting the nearby deep waters to overhear.

"Is that why you are frightened of the sea?" Jack studied me.

"No, maybe ... a little," I shrugged. "I don't want my name to be a prophecy."

"You don't have to be afraid anymore. The ocean is in my blood; I will always protect you. Goodnight my Ophelia, sleep well. I will be nearby."

And with that, he disappeared and my night ahead felt lonely.

ADAM

I'm sure I heard Ophelia speaking with someone when I went to get a glass of water from the kitchen around ten p.m. Soft voices drifted down from upstairs. I suppose it could have been the radio and I guess if Sebastian isn't worried I shouldn't be either, but I know guys my age and younger, and sneaking in to see a girl at night is not out of the question.

Seb's a good guy but he really is clueless in the parenting stakes. He thinks we're all flatmates which is great for me, but Lia has just come from a stable family environment and has never had this much freedom in her life; I feel the need to watch her back. Seb might not have done much that pushed the boundaries when he started dating, but when Vanessa and I hooked up in year ten we couldn't get enough of each other.

I snuck into her room so many nights that I can't believe we weren't caught. Then when her parents went away and she was supposed to be staying with her best friend, we stayed by ourselves at her house—it was a wild time and we did a few things that I wouldn't want my sister or Ophelia to do. I was also pretty persuasive to get my own way; I reckon a young guy will promise almost anything to impress and get the girl.

I hope it's not Chayse. The thought made me almost want to tear upstairs and check it out. I'd deck him something chronic if he was up there with her. I breathed deeply and let the thought go. Thinking of Vanessa made me miss her, but it was over, definitely over. My best mate Zach's girlfriend has a friend she wants to set me up with, so maybe this weekend.

OPHELIA

I slept so soundly that I surprised myself. I guess eventually the body overrides all longing and takes what it needs—sleep. The moment my head touched the pillow, my eyes could not stay open and I felt for just a few moments his cold lips on mine. I smiled and drifted into sleep.

Like my first day in Port Fairy, again I woke to Uncle Seb's voice yelling up the stairs. I glanced to the wall clock and it was five a.m. I couldn't believe I slept right through from ten p.m. last night until now! I heard Uncle Seb call out to me, and Argo and Agnes racing up the stairs to the attic.

Ship! I thought and jumped up, grabbing my dressing gown, pushing my hair sort of flat and racing up to join them.

Uncle Seb had his customary two cups of tea; he was lowered into one of the timber chairs and both dogs stood beside the window. Adam didn't join us on ship watch.

"Morning Lia, a ship is passing," he smiled excitedly.

"Morning Uncle Seb," I grinned back at him; his enthusiasm was kind of sweet. I hugged Argo and Agnes, then accepted the cup of tea. "Thank you." I looked out to the edge where the ocean disappeared. "Oh wow."

"She's a beauty isn't she?" Uncle Seb said and sipped his tea.

I nodded. "I can imagine why the early explorers thought the world was square and you could fall off the edge."

Uncle Seb laughed. "Indeed. Look at that horizon line, so sharp it could be drawn with a ruler and blue pen."

We sat watching as the ship coasted along the edge of the world and I wondered where Jack was now.

JACK

Ophelia was right, she will—like me—die a watery death.

Last night I watched her sleep for as long as I could—I wanted to lie beside her all night, but I too, needed to re-energise. I had to go home, to return to the La Bella from where I draw my strength. I know that divers see my ship as a fascinating wreck— they circle it, touching it and marvelling at how well-preserved she was lying in her watery grave. She's not filled and covered with sand like some of the other ships that share the water with us.

But I don't see their La Bella. For me, she exists in a time warp; she floats grandly on the ocean just offshore visible only to me and my crew. I always felt pride when I saw her and I still feel that way every time I return to her; I love my life at sea. The La Bella is my home in all her beauty and strength and she charges me. I roam her deck and walk amongst the rooms; they come to life as it was in 1905. You should see her when the three masts are up and full of air, billowing, the rigging making a noise that only sailors can describe.

I used to love coming into port and going ashore. The young ladies were always happy to see the visiting sailors, even young ones like me and I loved to roam the streets and see the different markets, foods and cultures. These days, I just stayed in the harbour. Sometimes I sit on the deck and watch the people going about their business onshore. I can hear the tapping of the divers and see the fisherman as they try their luck every day. I can't wait to bring Ophelia here to be with me, maybe to be with me forever.

Sometimes while roaming my La Bella I hear my name called and I race up to do the captain's bidding or I join the Quartermaster when he has time to teach me knots and splices or guides me on how to steer the ship. I do not wish to relive the punishment for I've been birched several times—caught smoking and one time for neglect of duty when I fell asleep when I shouldn't have. I've got the marks to prove it, but I got off lightly. We're not a naval ship so I only copped a few hits and trust me, that's enough to put you off doing it again.

I am not always alone; sometimes the lads join me on deck or I walk into the galley where the cook is doing his best to create a meal with the supplies he has. I can smell the familiar odour of salted beef and beer and am no stranger to the taste of canned food. It is like nothing has changed and I am living my life at sea as planned. It is hard when they leave, but they always do—they belong on the other side. Me, I can't ... I don't know why. For years I've sought the life I never had—to be loved and to belong. I've had other girlfriends, many girlfriends. They've taught me their ways and I confess it hasn't been easy to adapt to their change in speech and their change in clothing. They sometimes take offence that I wish them to cover more of their bodies or that I choose to protect them or do things for them. Odd this new world; but not Ophelia. So feminine but open to a strong man in her life. No-one in my century of looking for real love has been like Ophelia. Now she sleeps and I wait.

CHAPTER 22

OPHELIA

I never thought Friday and more importantly, Saturday night would come. The week dragged and it is all Jack's fault. Every night he met me, sometimes staying only for an hour, each time making sure I was in bed well before midnight. I protested, cried, refused to talk to him—two minutes was my longest and then I forgave him. He took charge and that's the way it was going to be. Infuriating! I wondered if he was punishing me for going to the dance tonight, but I promised Holly I would go with her and my new friends have been so good to me. Jack insisted I go, but I wonder.

At times a panic settled over me that I would never see him again, but I was getting better at moving out of that headspace. Of course I would survive, I'm strong, but I swear I will never, ever risk love again if that happens. Never.

Since I had most nights alone this week, I used the time to catch up on my school work, my friends in Brisbane via Facebook and sleep, even though a short visit from Jack every night would keep me awake for hours dreaming of him.

The only thing that kept me sane was that Jack promised me a date on Saturday night—a real date. He would come to the door, meet

Adam if he was home—Uncle Seb would be away at his conference—and take me out. He would tell me how we would be together forever.

I wonder if ghosts ate. Surely not, they wouldn't need to, but could they eat just to blend in? I realised I didn't know much about ghosts. I was pretty up on vampires and demons, but blindly ignorant about ghosts. I tried to do more ghost research but most of it was just sightings and hauntings. No-one owned up to having a ghost hanging with them or being in love with a ghost.

I had also thrown myself into my shipwreck assignment because it made me feel closer to Jack and it was due next week. Peggy said she would read it for me if I emailed it to her over the weekend and asked me to do the same for her. I wrote up Adam and Chayse's account, included my research and press clippings. I analysed the cause and effect. So sad to think many sailors died close to shore but unable to swim to save themselves and weighted down with heavy seafaring clothing. So sad to think of my Jack ...

Last night he gave me enough emotional food to feed on all the next day, maybe even longer. I had just turned off the light but left the curtains open—I liked the moonlight coming in. I propped my pillow up so I could see the moon as I dozed off and then I felt the chill—Jack! He appeared lying beside me.

"You're here," I grinned stupidly.

"Just to say goodnight," he said. He took my hand as we lay in the dark of my room lit by moonlight.

"What did you do all day?" I asked, "besides think of me."

He smiled. "That I did, all day. And I worked ... I'm preparing my home for you to see."

"When?" I asked eagerly.

"Soon," he responded. "I know what you did all day, I watched you."

"So you have me in sight and I have to go on memory. Hardly fair."

Jack turned side on to look at me. "There's a song that I play because it reminds me of you. It can be our song if you like it—you could play it if your memory needs topping up."

"What is it?" I asked expecting it to be some old song he had heard a hundred years ago.

"Where's your phone?" he leaned up and I handed it to him.

"You do it," he said. "I don't like the technology."

"Really?" I said. "I can't imagine life without it."

"That's because you've never lived without it," he reminded me. "Look up the band Hunters and Collectors. The song is '*Throw your arms around me*'."

I smiled at the title and quickly found it.

"Listen to it with me," Jack said as he rolled onto his back again, took my free hand and closed his eyes.

I started the song and closed my eyes too. The lyrics brought tears to my eyes.

And then he was gone again.

HOLLY

I had spread the word that Lia wasn't interested in Chayse, that she had met someone who didn't go to our school and I made sure it went to Imogen's group. It seemed to work as we didn't get any more letters or trouble, but that didn't stop Imogen still looking towards our group on the bus like we all had leprosy.

But now I had Chayse sussing me for information about Lia. Who was she seeing? Was she seeing Adam? Plus, telling me how he hated Adam and on it went. It's not hurting my reputation having Chayse Johann talking to me, but he looks right through me and if he can't see me and Lia's not interested then, um, see you later Chayse!

In the last class for Friday afternoon, I had a study break in the library and Chayse's class was in there too. I looked up as he pulled a chair next to me. Chayse doesn't seem to realise that half of the girls in year eleven and twelve—including me—are tongue-tied around him.

"Ha, you're doing the history assignment," he scoffed recognising it from my Word document on the screen.

I nodded like an idiot. I managed to get out my topic. "I'm investigating whether the digital age will change our view on history."

Chayse looked impressed, yeah, go me.

"And will it?" he asked.

I shrugged and there goes the impressed look. I tried to save myself. "It will definitely change how we record it and may change how we perceive it as we have more views and opinions to access."

A nod and an impressed look returned to his face again. I'm on a roll.

"How's Lia's assignment coming along ... on the shipwreck cause and history?" he asked. Didn't take him long to get back to Lia.

"Good," I said, "I think she's nearly finished."

"Did Adam tell her about the curse?" he asked.

I shook my head. To be honest, I didn't know if he had or not, but I was so taken in by his tall, blondeness—is that even a word?—that I didn't want to talk, I wanted him to talk and talk and stay near me. I pulled myself together but noticed several of the girls in the class were looking at me with nothing short of envy.

"What is the curse?" I prodded him to tell me about it, even though I knew.

Chayse smiled. "Well the legend goes that if any of the survivors —that's obviously the descendants now—or anyone who was even remotely connected with the La Bella is near the ocean late at night, then the La Bella crew reclaim them for their own and they have to serve on the ship with them forever! Great, huh?" he grinned.

I think I shuddered and then I found my voice.

"No, it's truly creepy and awful given it was an accident," I said, forgetting that I was in awe of him.

Chayse shrugged, indifferent to my thoughts. "I guess it is creepy."

"Why would the deceased seek revenge?" I continued. "It's not like they were deserted, everyone tried to help but it was impossible."

"Maybe they don't bear a grudge," Chayse said, "after all the sailors knew the risk and how dangerous the sea can be. Maybe they just want to all be together again and they don't realise they are dead … it's kind of a freaky ghost story," he stopped to reflect.

I nodded, wide-eyed and encouraging.

"Yeah, it's kind of kinship," he decided.

"Then why is it called a curse?" I asked.

"Fair point," Chayse nodded. "Anyway, Adam should be careful." He tapped my arm and rose. "Been good talking with you Holly." And then he was gone and so was I—physically and mentally. He remembered my name.

OPHELIA

Uncle Seb was away at his conference but Adam offered to drop Holly, Harry and me to the dance tonight before he went out with his friends. Peggy's mother was dropping her to the dance and picking her up at ten p.m. sharp. Adam said he'd swing by and grab us at eleven which was pretty good of him to cut his night short to pick up three schoolies. He was a good soul.

I came downstairs and saw Adam, Argo and Agnes waiting in the lounge room. Adam looked good in his jeans and black shirt. He gave a low whistle on seeing me and Agnes barked.

"This old thing," I grinned. The house shuddered and I looked skywards at its two 'eye' windows and thanked it too. "Now you two be good kids," I said giving Argo and Agnes a pat. I turned to Adam. "Ready?"

"Yep," Adam said, reaching for his car keys. "You look really lovely."

"Thank you," I said. I left my hair down, put on a bit of make-up—mainly mascara because I didn't have much make-up. I used to borrow some of Mum's every now and then when I snuck out but there was no-one to borrow from in this house. Also, in defiance of my last few horrendous months, I didn't want to wear anything black; I had had enough of black so I wore my sequinned A-line, silver party dress that Mum had bought me for our year ten end of school dance back home. It was long-sleeved and the length came to just above my knees and was very girly, but that's just fine by me. I had matching silver sandals and a bag.

Adam ensured Argo and Agnes were secure in the house and within minutes we were pulling up outside Holly and Harry's place. Mrs Geers greeted us and took a thousand photos.

"It's only a school dance, Mum, not the graduation formal," Holly rolled her eyes.

"I know but you all look so beautiful," she continued to take photos—Holly and Harry; Holly and I; me and Harry; the three of us; the three of us with Adam; Holly and Harry with their Mum; and just when the cat was about to get a look in, we made a break for it.

As we pulled out of their driveway, Holly turned back from waving goodbye to her mother.

"I told Mum that you were picking us up, Adam, but she did her hair and makeup anyway just because Sebastian might come too," Holly shook her head.

"He's away for a week at a conference," I told Holly.

Adam glanced at Holly in his rear-view mirror. "Well, you look lovely, Holly—that jade dress does bring out the green in your eyes," he teased her. "You scrubbed up okay too, Harry."

"Yeah thanks," he smiled. "Chic magnet, what can you do?"

"It's a burden we must bear," Adam agreed.

I shook my head at the two of them. I couldn't believe I was here in Victoria, going to a dance with three people in the car who I didn't know three months ago and that somewhere out there, watching, was a guy I was madly in love with. Life was truly bizarre. I missed him and my hand went involuntarily to my heart. I glanced out the window, only seeing my own reflection. In the background, I could hear the three of them laughing and talking. I suddenly felt totally alone.

Adam nudged me and I came back to reality and got back into the conversation.

"What's the dance theme?" Adam asked.

"Written in the stars," Holly said. "I was supposed to be on the committee but in the end, there were too many involved and no-one could agree on anything so I dropped out."

I loved the theme, it made me think of Jack and our love. Although pretty much everything made me think of Jack.

We arrived at the school hall and Adam pulled the car to the shoulder next to the footpath for us to alight. I could see the hall was well lit outside, dimly lit inside with hundreds of stars dangling from the ceiling at different heights, the music pumped already. Everyone looked so different all glammed-up and further along Imogen and her group were heading inside. I wanted to make sure I was nowhere near them.

"Have a good time and behave ... Harry," Adam joked.

"For sure. Thanks for the ride, appreciate it," Harry hit Adam on the shoulder as he piled out.

"I just need to talk to Lia for a minute," Adam said.

"We'll loiter and thank you, Adam," Holly said ever so sweetly. She's so transparent. I waited with my hand on the door handle while Holly made a face at me and closed the door.

"Are you okay?" Adam looked at me.

"Sure, of course. Why?" I frowned at him. I was rubbing the top of my bag nervously. What did he know?

"You looked a little sad for a moment there, like you weren't with us," he said.

He had seen my hand on my heart.

"I'm good, great even," I exaggerated, fussing with my dress.

Adam turned to face me and put his arm across the back of my seat. I looked straight ahead not wanting to meet his eyes.

"Lia, you've been through a lot and it's okay to be a bit overwhelmed by stuff," he shrugged. "I'm no expert on loss, not by any means, but I'm here, okay?"

I nodded. "Thanks, I really appreciate it."

"Then look at me," he said.

I turned to look at him. His eyes scanned my face.

"I'll see you at eleven, huh? But call me if you need me earlier."

"Thanks," I nodded. I opened the door and bolted. Close call ... I thought he'd stumbled on something about Jack. I caught up with Harry and Holly as Peggy's mum pulled their car to the kerb.

"Go do your thing, tiger," I teased Harry.

He smirked at me but looked quite handsome in dress shirt and pants. He wandered over to meet Mrs Carboney.

At the side of the building I saw Chayse talking with Imogen—might be on again. I felt bad for Imogen—who wanted to love someone when it wasn't returned.

"Let's go gorgeous." I looped arms with my date, Holly, and we headed inside.

HOLLY

It was great to see Ophelia chilled and up; so different from the Ophelia that arrived at school—the new girl—not that long ago. It was great for me too, like we'd been thrown together when both of our circumstances changed. After ten years hanging around with my two best friends at school, I couldn't believe they could both leave after year ten. It just sucks, but then along comes Ophelia and we get each other. I know she would rather be with Jack than with me at the dance, so it said a lot about friendship that she came along.

We walked in the hallway and the theme committee had done a great job; the place just glimmered.

"This is great," she said circling in the light, the bling on her dress sparkling.

"Let's dance," I grabbed her arm as one of my favourite songs came on. We weaved away into the middle where we could dance without being on show. Harry and Peggy joined us and I had to hand it to Harry, he could move okay. I wouldn't be telling him that though. We must have stayed there for about six or seven songs straight and then a slow song came on. Our cue to go!

∼

OPHELIA

It felt good to dance again; I hadn't done it since the year ten end of school dance in Brisbane, before all the drama. The dance floor was already half-packed when we got on and right under the largest, glittering star, Imogen was dancing with Chayse. She looked in our direction and smirked. Jack had nothing on Imogen when it came to cold fronts. Brrr! Jack again, sigh, can't get him out of my head and don't want to. Peggy looked like she had died and gone to heaven with Harry. She looked gorgeous, even Harry was more attentive to her than usual.

As soon as a slow song came on Holly grabbed my arm and we got out of there. Harry stayed and had a dance with Peggy, and Imogen had her arms around Chayse's neck so fast he didn't get a chance to bolt. He gave me a strange look—kind of resigned to his girlfriend fate. He could just be without a girlfriend for a while or ask out any one of the other ten girls standing watching him from the corners of the room.

"Let's go outside for some air," I said to Holly above the music. She was about to follow me when one of the guys from our English class—whose name escapes me—asked her to dance. She looked at me and I gave her an encouraging wave and headed out. I saw another guy I recognised heading towards me and I slipped out before I had to make excuses.

I was kind of pleased to have a minute alone, I wanted to think about Jack. I moved away from the hall, past the dance monitors—also known as sucked-in parents—who were dealing with a senior guy they had caught smoking and a couple about to go way past the kissing phase. I slipped around the side of the building and leaning against it, closed my eyes. It was dark and cool and I was far enough away that the music was muted, just the bass thumped on.

"You look beautiful."

I gasped and opened my eyes. My hand raced to my heart.

"I'm sorry," Jack stepped back, his hands up in a surrender motion. "I didn't mean to frighten you."

"You nearly gave me a heart attack," I gasped, "I thought I was alone."

"You're never alone, anymore," he smiled. "Does that freak you out?"

I drank in the sight of Jack in a dark suit, crisp white shirt and blue tie. His black dress shoes were highly polished and his hair groomed and slicked back. He was gorgeous, his blue eyes searing through me with his gaze.

"Nothing about you freaks me out at all," I said. "You dressed for tonight."

"Couldn't let you down when you look so very beautiful," he said taking my hands and standing back to look at me.

"So beautiful," he whispered.

I could feel myself blushing and tingling from my toes to my fingers to my scalp. I moved towards him and he cupped my face in his hands. I looked up into his eyes and he moved in slowly and kissed me. It was truly amazing I remained standing for the feelings that overwhelmed me. At last, I felt secure again, so much better—I didn't realise just how anxious I had been from being away from him. He drew me into a tight embrace and I could feel his strength and his relief too. It was palpable.

"Did I mention that I am a great dancer," he said.

I pulled away and grinned at him.

"No you did not ... show me your moves," I teased him. "Hold on ... what sort of dances did they do over a hundred years ago?"

"Dances where they held the girl very close and the man led," he said. "Like this."

He took my hand in his, placed a hand on my back and to the beat of the slower music playing in the hall, we danced. He really did lead, I danced well just following him and I've never really learned to waltz or any of those more formal dances.

"I love you, Ophelia," he whispered in my ear as he glided me around our own dance floor.

"I love you, Jack, forever," I said and then he dipped me, powerfully holding me.

"Now you need to get back to the dance," he righted me again.

"They won't miss me," I said.

"They will. I would. Tomorrow we have a date and I will pick you up at your front door at seven p.m. Come dressed for a beach picnic under the stars."

I think I squealed with excitement and Jack laughed.

"It's been an awful week without you, Jack."

"I've been there the whole time," he said, "and I gave you signs I was there, beside you," Jack pressed me against the wall and my heartbeat raced.

"I know," I said, "and I needed that, but I want you in the flesh."

He grimaced at the term and I backtracked.

"In spirit, in form, anyway, I just want you," I touched his cool skin. "Jack, can I ask you something?"

"Okay," he agreed.

I hesitated but during my week of missing him, my doubts had risen. I swallowed.

"When you weren't with me, were you with someone else?"

Anger flared in Jack's face and he stepped back.

"No," I grabbed his suit jacket and pushed myself in front of him again. "I love you Jack but I have to ask you that."

And then he was gone.

"No," I called to the air, to the sky. "Jack," I hissed, angry now. "Come back here. You at least owe me this assurance, it's not a lot to ask, unless you do have something to hide," I crossed my arms.

Then I heard a soft laugh. I spun around and he wasn't there.

"I'm going back to the dance," I threatened in a sing-song voice.

Again the chuckle behind me. I turned and he still hadn't appeared.

"Okay then, I'll see you tomorrow if you're just going to play around." I began to walk off and he appeared, grabbed my arm and pulled me back.

Jack smiled. "Ah, Ophelia, how could you ask me that?"

"And yet, you haven't answered," I reminded him as I straightened his tie. He smiled down at me, holding all the power, all the cards again and he knew it.

"I have waited a century for you, Ophelia. Why would I throw that away on a whim? You are the one, the only one—and of those I have known in the past um ... decades, as Hamlet said to his Ophelia, 'I love thee best, O most best, believe it'."

I smiled and all was well in the world again. "Okay, you can go now," I dismissed him.

Jack laughed; pulled me closer and kissed me long and hard. When he pulled away, I was breathless.

"Lia, YOU can go now," he said, granting me permission.

I stepped back, dizzy and happy.

"Aren't you going to ... you know ... vanish?" I watched him.

He shook his head. "Nope. I want to watch you walk away in that dress."

I smiled and turned. I walked away feeling his eyes on my back. At the edge of the building, I turned back and he stood, hands in his pockets, rocking on his heels, looking breathtakingly beautiful and somehow, I tore myself away, turned and returned to the dance.

∾

ADAM

Great, just what I needed. I pulled up in my 4WD to pick up Lia, Harry and Holly and who should be on the footpath outside the school dance but Chayse Johann. I drove along further; not that I was worried about an encounter with that idiot, but I didn't want to ruin Lia's night. I turned off the car, stayed seated behind the wheel but I could see him watching me.

I was five minutes early but I glanced to the hall; Lia and Holly were heading down the path to wait for me, Harry was right behind them.

Sure enough, Chayse made his way over—he managed to tear himself away from whatever swooning female was clinging to him at the time and swaggered my way. I ignored him and he knocked on my driver's window door. Instead of putting it down, I opened the door.

"You want something?" I asked. He was dressed up in a suit and standing with his arms folded.

"Just wanted to remind you about the midnight curse," he smirked.

"Going to enforce it yourself?" I laughed and his eyes narrowed. I continued: "Listen schoolie, move along, I'm not here for you. Get back to class."

I knew that would piss him off and it did. He grabbed my shirt, pulled me out of the car and slammed me up against the door. In my peripheral vision, I saw Ophelia running towards us in her party dress as fast as her heels would allow, with Holly in pursuit.

"Chayse, leave him alone," she ran up to us.

"Got Ophelia fighting your battles now?" he smiled.

I gave him a hard push, enough to send him stumbling. Luckily there was no coming traffic but it hurt his pride and he steadied himself, ready for action.

I opened the back car door. "Get in ladies," I ordered Ophelia and Holly. Harry came and stood next to me.

"Hey Chayse, good night huh?" he tried to pacify the situation.

Chayse looked at him then back at me. A group had now gathered, the dance monitors or whatever they called them were not aware, yet.

"Chayse, please, don't ruin my night," Ophelia said.

"Get in the car," I told her again, and then I don't know what happened, but I felt this cold feeling and the next thing I knew, Chayse was on the ground again and Ophelia was in the back seat, but she had sort of fallen in which was kind of weird given Holly was beside her and still standing. It was like she had been lifted and pushed in.

I didn't have time to think about it because I was keeping my eyes on Chayse. His mate Tyler showed up, gave him a hand up and took him away with a nod to the girls. I watched them walk away. I didn't lay a hand on him and I didn't see Lia do so either but there he was sprawled and down for the count.

"Let's go, Adam, please," Ophelia said.

"Are you both okay?" I asked Lia and Holly. They nodded, I closed their door, got in the driver's seat and Harry jumped in the front passenger seat beside me.

"Thanks, Harry," I muttered.

"No problem, he's a stirrer, don't know why he just didn't stay with his group," Harry said.

"I'm sorry, Adam," Ophelia said.

I indicated and pulled out to drive us home.

"No, I'm sorry Lia and Holly. Honestly, I didn't provoke that, I was just sitting in the car. I wouldn't have embarrassed you at your dance."

"You've got a good right though mate," Harry said with a grin.

I smiled. I do, but I don't remember using it.

CHAPTER 23

OPHELIA

It was just after eight on Saturday morning when there was a knock on the front door. I was up because I couldn't sleep—I was too excited about my date with Jack that night. Uncle Seb wasn't due home until later that day, besides he had his own key. Who would drop in at this hour? Argo and Agnes started up a chorus of barking; I waited but Adam didn't appear so by the second knock I raced down the stairs to see who was there.

I opened the door and beside me, Argo and Agnes settled immediately wagging their tails, they knew our visitor—our very attractive visitor. She was a bit taller than me, had fire red hair that fell in waves down to her waist, green eyes and a smattering of freckles.

"Hello Argo and Agnes!" she greeted them before looking at me. "Hello, you must be Ophelia, I'm Vanessa."

Ah, so this was Vanessa. Adam's ex. Yep, she was something.

I took her offered hand, shook it and invited her in.

"It's good to meet you," I said. "I'd offer you a tea or something, but I'm guessing you're here to see Adam?"

"I am, but thanks. How are you settling in?" she asked, which was nice.

"Much better than I thought," I said honestly.

She smiled. "Well, that's a bonus."

"I can see if Adam is in ... " I glanced down the hallway.

"That's cool, I know the way," she said. "Good to meet you."

"You too." I watched her stride confidently down the hall. She had done this before. Argo and Agnes looked at me expectantly.

"Okay, I'll get changed," I told them.

I called after her. "Can you let Adam know I'm taking the dogs for a w-a-l-k," I spelled the word out so they wouldn't go berserk with excitement before I got changed into beach gear.

"Sure," she laughed and with a quick knock on his door, walked straight into Adam's room. At the same time, Adam must have heard our voices and appeared at the door just as she knocked. He wore only a pair of fitted black boxer shorts with a white Calvin Klein band around the top, and nothing else. I quickly looked away but he had an impressive six-pack happening.

I raced upstairs, put on a T-shirt, hoodie and jogging shorts so I could wade ankle-deep in the cold, shallow water as we walked—that was sure to invigorate me. I slid a hairband around my wrist.

At the foot of the stairs, Argo and Agnes joined me. I heard raised voices from the bedroom, so we hurriedly slipped out the front door, crossed the cul de sac, passed a small silver Mazda which must have been Vanessa's, and then we were on the beach.

I loved the first impact of the sand between my toes and the sight of the ocean—I can't believe I spent my life without it. This morning, the beach was crisp and clean, the surfers were out in force, and Argo, Agnes and I walked along happily lost in our thoughts.

I didn't expect to see or feel Jack today, I knew he would stay away from me until our date tonight to heighten the longing and it did—I was aching to see him again. I wonder if we became an official couple how much he could be in my world. Could he stay with me at night? Could he come to dances? Could he hang with my friends or would he always have to be hidden or a secret? Would he have to recharge—sort of like a vampire staying out of the light all day?

We walked along and greeted some of the other walkers and their dogs that we had come to recognise. I could see some surfers in the distance; they weren't close enough to work out if Chayse was amongst them... maybe Imogen was on the beach too if he got back with her last night at the dance. Then my thoughts drifted to Adam and Vanessa and I wondered why they had broken up. I wasn't in that space for long; as always my thoughts returned to Jack. I glanced behind at our rock, but he was not there. I smiled because tonight, I knew we would both be.

$\sim$

HOLLY

I liked Peggy and even though I didn't really know her that well before Lia started at the school, I liked her a lot less when she rang me at eight o'clock on Saturday morning!

"What are you doing ringing at eight on Saturday? Why are you awake?" I yawned.

"Oh, sorry," she mumbled. "I didn't know people weren't up at this time."

I began to laugh because that was truly the weirdest statement ever and she joined in.

"It's fine," I assured her when we stopped laughing. "How was your date with Harry and don't tell me the gory details."

"Um, then how can I put this ... it was a dream come true," Peggy said.

I groaned. "Well I'm delighted for you but I can't imagine my brother making that happen."

"Aren't twins supposed to be close?" she asked.

"Allegedly, but he was stealing my oxygen in the womb and he's still stealing my music and my ... never mind," I stopped. "But on the subject of my brother, if you want my advice, some of the girls in our class are more worried about losing their phones then their virginity..." I heard Peggy gasp. "You're so not like that I know, so if he doesn't look after you, let me know! You looked great last night by the way."

"Thanks," she said. "And thanks for caring." I could hear her blushing.

"Sure," I said.

There was a moment's silence while I opened the curtains and I waited for Peggy to talk. "Not that it's not great to hear from you, but did you want to talk to me about something?" I eventually prompted.

"Oh yes, sorry, I got distracted thinking about Harry," she said.

I shook my head. *Really?*

Peggy continued. "I'm wondering if you remember the name of Lia's boyfriend?"

That question took me by surprise. I dropped back on the end of the bed and fell back into it. "Mm, Jack," I said. "I think he snuck into the dance last night because she came back inside pretty happy."

"Jack," Peggy said. "Do you remember his last name?"

"Yes ... let me think," I closed my eyes and thought hard. "It was something like Denim."

"Denham?" Peggy asked.

"That sounds right," I agreed. "Jack Denham. She only told me his full name once but I tried to remember it to see if Harry or Mum knew of him. Harry meets a lot of guys our age with cycling and sports stuff."

I heard Peggy draw a deep breath. "Holly, I know what you're thinking, well what you are going to be thinking, but ..." she hesitated.

"What am I going to be thinking?" I hesitantly asked Peggy.

"In a minute you are going to be thinking that I'm really strange."

"Oh is that all," I sighed with relief. "I already think that," I told her.

"Do you?" she sounded really surprised.

"No! I'm joking," I assured her. It was way too early for this conversation, I should be sleeping. "Go ahead, tell me."

"Well, it's just that ... promise this will stay between us?" she pleaded.

"Okay I promise." I was now getting concerned. I sat upright. "What's up?"

"Well it's probably nothing but Lia sent me her assignment, we swapped to proof each other's work, and well, it's silly but she mentions a guy called Jack Denham."

"So ..." I followed along.

"Jack Denham died on the La Bella in 1905."

I stood and went to the window, looking out as I took in what Peggy was saying. The neighbour was about to start his mower and Harry was washing Dad's car, probably to try and persuade him to take him out for some 'L' driving time. He still needed forty more hours of supervised learners' driving practice time for his licence.

"Holly?" Peggy said, "are you there?"

"Sorry, yes I was thinking," I answered. "There's probably a thousand Jack Denham's around, I told her. But it's a weird coincidence I guess. I saw her Jack when he was in the grandstand during art class; she pointed him out to me."

"There's a picture of the 1905 Jack in her assignment," Peggy said.

There was silence on the line.

"Do you want me to email it to you?" Peggy asked.

"Yes, please," I said.

I heard the ping go off as I was talking on the phone. "I'll open it on my laptop and email you back."

"Thanks, I know what you're thinking ... the idea is crazy," Peggy said. "Talk soon then?"

"Absolutely," I agreed with a chuckle that bordered a little on wary and hysterical. "Hey, don't worry, I'm sure it's just one of those weird coincidences. They might look alike cause they're related ... if he's an ancestor of Jack's, you know..."

I hung up and went to my laptop, logging in. Opening my emails I clicked on the photo attached to Peggy's and it took up the whole screen.

I stared at the photo, then I had to sit down.

OPHELIA

I stayed out as long as I could to give Adam some privacy. It wasn't too difficult—the dogs and I were enjoying our morning watching the world go by on the beach and I was planning what I would wear tonight, and dreaming of kissing Jack again. Last night was so romantic, even if we only had fifteen minutes together. Speaking of last night, I looked over at the surfers but Chayse wasn't amongst them at my end of the beach. I wondered how his night had ended.

After a good hour of watching the morning go by and texting friends, I was just about to rouse the dogs who lay beside me on the sand to head home when Adam appeared down near our entrance path to the beach. He went to the water's edge but didn't go in. He looked up and down the beach; I think he was looking for me. I called out and waved and he jogged over.

"Hey, great day," he said dropping down beside us.

I agreed. He looked towards the surfers.

"You're safe, I'm pretty sure Chayse isn't here," I told him.

He scoffed like he didn't care. "I was checking out the wave size."

"Oh right," I said, only half convinced.

He turned to me. "You don't have to stay out of our house just because someone drops in, but thanks for that anyway."

I shrugged. "It's all good. We were just enjoying it here, weren't we kids? Time sort of gets away from you."

He nodded and looked out to sea. I subtly studied him and I think it is fair to say he was cheesed off. His jaw was locked and he frowned and fidgeted.

"Vanessa's quite beautiful," I said.

"Yeah and she knows it," he snapped back.

"Well, she seemed nice."

"She's a nutter."

Right, I let that go.

He rubbed his hand over his eyes and then looked over at me.

"Sorry Lia, I shouldn't take my frustration out on you. I wish she would just get on with her life and leave me out of it," he looked back to sea.

I didn't know if I was supposed to ask questions, nod sympathetically or say something consoling. I looked to Argo and Agnes who looked away—smart! I took a stab at it.

"You don't want to be with her then?" I asked.

"I did once. She was two-timing me and I caught her out. Then she dropped him because she wanted to be with me, but what's the point?" he shook his head. "I wasn't enough for her the first time for whatever reason."

"What was the reason, did she tell you?" I asked gently.

Adam dug his feet into the cold sand and moved the sand around as he spoke. "We had been going out since the start of year ten—about three years—but last year she said she didn't want to settle down too early with a boyfriend when there's so many fish in the sea," he shrugged. "I understand that, there are other chicks I'd like to go out with too, but what do you do if you're in love with someone even if you are young? If you give it up to try other things and realise it was right, then you may lose your way back to each other."

I wrapped my arms around my legs and rested my chin on my knees. "That's a sad thought," I said. "But what if you got to thirty years old and all you've ever known is one love, is it enough? Would you feel like you were missing out?" I asked him.

"Maybe," he agreed.

I continued: "But then again, some people never find a great love and what if you spent a decade looking for that person and you had it the first time and threw it away?"

"Exactly," he said. "I'm not saying she was the one, but I didn't think we'd run our course yet, that's all. I didn't see it coming and she could have called it off before she started seeing someone else."

I thought about Jack—I couldn't bear to lose him, not now, not in the future.

"So does she want to get back together?" I asked.

"Yeah, every now and then she drops in and wants to talk about it. Says she's made a big mistake, whatever."

"But you don't want to try again?"

He shook his head. "I've been through all that drama—betrayal and break up. Why would I risk it again with Vanessa? Geez, she can't be loyal for three years, what hope have we got long-term? Nuh, she was right the first time, it's time to move on, for both of us."

We sat in silence for a while. I silently prayed Jack would love me forever and never feel like that. I hoped his words to me about waiting for me for a century were true and not just words he said to win my heart.

"Well, you're a good catch big brother, it's her loss," I said.

He smiled but didn't look at me. "Thanks."

"C'mon," I nudged him, "I'll make you my world-famous scrambled eggs for breakfast. Argo and Agnes will love them too."

Adam grinned. "Should I pick up a burger?"

"Shut up!" I hit his arm indignantly. "You wait, you'll be asking for my recipe."

He rose, extended his hand and pulled me up, and the four of us went home.

CHAPTER 24

OPHELIA

*A*fter breakfast which Adam said was really good, he moped around for the rest of the morning. He disappeared a couple of times in his car, came back and went for a surf. I was home the whole time—my books, laptop and pens sprawled over the large kitchen table as I caught up on school work. Argo and Agnes kept me company until another knock at the door just before two o'clock. I jumped up and opened it to find Holly and Peggy there.

"Hey you two," I said really pleased to see them. "Come in."

They were both in jeans and pullovers; we didn't see each other out of school uniform much. Argo and Agnes were excited to meet Peggy and after they settled down, I led Holly and Peggy through the house.

"What's happening?" I asked.

Peggy looked nervous and glanced at Holly. I frowned at them both.

"Okay, you're worrying me," I said.

"No, it's just a social visit, sort of," Holly said.

"I'm bringing back your assignment, I printed it out and just marked two changes," Peggy said.

"Ah thanks, I'm almost done reading yours—so good," I told her, and looked from one to the other; there was definitely something going on.

"Come through," I invited them into the huge galley kitchen and offered them a drink. We sat around the wide bench—Holly took a Diet Coke and Peggy took up the offer of tea. I put the jug on and grabbed two cups to join her.

"Adam not in?" Holly looked around.

"No, he's having a surf," I smiled at her. "But stick around long enough and he'll be back. I met Vanessa this morning."

"Ooh," Holly's eyes widened. "What did you think?"

"She's lovely—pretty and nice," I said.

"I remember her," Peggy said. "They were always a very attractive couple."

"Hot," Holly agreed. "Vanessa would be in senior at our school if she hadn't talked her parents into letting her go to a school that focussed on the performing arts. Are they back on?"

I shook my head. "I think she broke Adam's heart and he isn't prepared to let her have two goes at it—well that's my understanding of it."

I finished adding milk to our teas, pushed one to Peggy and sat down with them.

"It's so cosy in here," Peggy looked at the dogs lying in the lounge room in a ray of sun as it streamed through the crystal-shaped windows.

"So, what's up?" I asked again, "not that you can't just drop around without a reason."

Peggy looked to Holly again. "It's about Jack," she started.

I bristled at the mention of Jack. He was mine and not up for discussion, yet.

"Oh," I tried to sound casual, "he dropped into the dance last night, you know, just for a while. I would have introduced you if you had come out."

Holly nodded. "When are you seeing him again?"

"Tonight, why?" I asked surprised.

"It's just that ... well, I'm worried about how much you know about him," Holly said.

"Enough," I assured them. I wanted this discussion to be over.

Peggy stepped in again. "It's just that I thought you told me his name was Jack Denham and in your assignment, there's a Jack Denham." Peggy looked at my assignment on the table between us.

"Right," I nodded. I knew where they were going with this but I wasn't going to make it easy.

"And your Jack and that Jack who drowned out there," Peggy nodded towards the ocean, "they look alike, a lot alike," she nervously sipped her tea.

I looked from Holly to Peggy and said: "you know how insane you sound don't you?"

They both nodded.

"So you think my Jack is the Jack from my assignment who died on the La Bella and would now be close to 130 years old?" I narrowed my eyes and looked at them.

Peggy giggled at how absurd it sounded.

Holly nodded. "Yeah, it does sound out there when you say it like that. But we just want to be sure you're okay, Lia. There are girls who have died in this town because they've drowned and some say it is an accident and some say, well other things. I'm just saying if you're not careful and don't know your way around, well, you can't trust everyone ..."

I nodded again. "Thanks. I really appreciate that you are worried about me."

We sat in awkward silence. I had gotten away with it because neither Peggy nor Holly had directly asked me if my Jack was ... sounds weird, a ghost or dead ... so I didn't have to answer.

"Did you come down from Warrnambool just to ask me that?" I said to Peggy.

She nodded. "It's okay, I just took the bus."

"You're sweet," I squeezed her hand. I was keen to change the subject in case they came back to it. I was saved by the bell as the phone began to ring. At the same time, the front door opened and Adam yelled out "I'll get it."

I saw Holly brighten. I heard him answer and chat for a few moments before hanging up. He came into the kitchen in his board shorts, a towel around his shoulder and no shirt. His hair was mussed up and he looked fit and tanned—it didn't go unnoticed.

"Hey Holly, and you must be Peggy," he said.

"I am," Peggy said shyly. "Thanks for offering to pick me up the other night but Mum, well she's insanely strict."

Adam shrugged. "No problem."

"Speaking of insane," I said to Adam, "aren't you freezing? It's officially winter after all."

"You're soft Lia," he teased. "Makes you feel alive that cold water. I'm making a coffee, anyone?"

We all declined. Adam pulled the towel from around his shoulders and slipped on his hoodie that lay draped over a kitchen chair. He continued: "That was Sebastian on the phone. They've asked him to stay a few more days."

On cue, the house howled. Peggy and Holly both jumped; Adam, the dogs and I didn't react.

"What was that?" Holly's eyes were huge.

"Just the house," I said.

"The wind ... the design of the house and our location makes it howl sometimes," Adam explained stirring sugar into his coffee.

"That's freaky," Peggy said.

I looked up at the house and smiled. "And kind of cool too, I said." Adam smiled at me, we were thinking the same thing—our house was missing Seb.

"Anyway, he should be home Tuesday but said he'd call you later, Lia, when you were alone."

"Thanks," I nodded. It was good Holly and Peggy were there, a nice distraction, otherwise, I would have been way too anxious waiting all day for my date tonight.

"So what are you three up to?" Adam asked.

I shrugged, "we're just hanging out." I looked at Holly and then to Peggy and they nodded their agreement.

"But I have to go; I've got study to do," Peggy added.

Adam narrowed his eyes. "Mm, there's some plotting going on, I can tell."

"Us?" Holly asked with exaggerated innocence.

Adam grinned. "I'll leave you to it. I've got to shower and head to Zach's place."

I brightened. "Zach who lives in Warrnambool?"

"Yeah, want a ride?" he asked.

"No, but Peggy could use a lift if that's okay?" I asked.

"Just to the train or city if that works for you, please?" Peggy asked. "I'll get home from there. If you drop me home I'll be grounded until I'm twenty."

"I can do that," Adam said. "I'll be ready in fifteen minutes."

"Thank you, big brother," I said sweetly.

"Yeah, yeah," he rolled his eyes and left. Holly looked particularly disappointed that she lived just down the road.

JACK

Night was falling and my strength was growing. In one hour I would be with Ophelia, my beautiful Ophelia. Yet, I sensed she was falling for Adam ... she looks at him with great affection and calls him brother, they are getting closer. I can't lose her to him and tonight I will re-establish our bond.

This week while she slept and schooled, I have been preparing for her—doing up the Captain's quarters which are mine now as I am the only one who lives forever on the ship. You should see it; I know she will love it. I have replicated the room that she loves so much at her home—scrubbed and polished floors, filled with white furnishings and linens, highly-polished timber and of course, the view from each window is the blue-green waters of the port.

The lower and upper quarter decks are spotless; are as clean as they have ever been. The rigging and sails neatly hung and stored. I even buffed the bell on the main mast. The La Bella feels like a romantic escape at sea for two. I can't wait to see her on it, to give her a tour and welcome her to her new home.

CHAPTER 25

OPHELIA

I went to the front door, moved away again and returned to the lounge room. I didn't want to look too eager, but it was nearly seven p.m. and I was waiting for Jack's knock on the door—unless he just appeared. I looked around, nope. I had walked Argo and Agnes and given them their dinner. They had completed their dusk rounds of the property and, content that all was well, had settled into their usual positions in the lounge room.

The house moaned, it had been moaning for over an hour now—I didn't know how to console it. Adam was not home yet, he may even stay at Zach's and Uncle Seb was away so Jack's kind gesture to meet the family wasn't going to happen.

I had a few things ready to stick into a picnic basket because Jack said it would be a beach picnic but I wasn't sure what he could eat or even if he would eat. I tried shopping for a ghost and when that didn't work I shopped for a sailor. I bought some things that he might be used to eating like seafood, cheese, a breadstick and I bought chocolate and soft drink, why not? I packed them and then unpacked them because I didn't know if he would want them.

Then I spent hours, and I mean hours, working out what to wear.

I wanted to look romantic—kind of ethereal—Jack likes feminine, but I had to be able to sit on the sand or a rock too. I sighed; guys just don't get how hard it is sometimes. Fine for them to say 'see you at seven for a beach picnic.' I chose a flowing cream skirt that went to my ankles, with petticoat layers underneath and a fitted pale blue cardigan with small pearl buttons. I had cream ballet slippers on my feet and I left my hair loose for the night. I knew I was a bit well-dressed for the beach, but it felt comfortable and romantic and I didn't care if I got sand or water on my skirt.

Finally a knock at the door. Argo and Agnes jumped up and beat me there; the hair on their back was standing up alert. Argo began to growl.

"It's okay Argo and Agnes," I assured them and closed the lounge door keeping them inside just until I had shown Jack around.

I opened the door and Jack was there looking divine. He wore a dark suit and an open-neck white shirt, no tie. He held one dozen long stem white roses, the most dramatic bouquet I had ever seen and my first bouquet.

Both dogs barked from the other side of the door and the house wailed. Jack ignored it, moved forward and placing an arm around my waist, drew me to him. He stopped short of kissing me, oblivious to the calamity around us and looked at me.

"Ophelia, you take my breath away," he said and then he kissed me.

The aching in my chest just got worse; I understood now how people died of heartbreak. If he left me now I would not be able to go on. I heard him moan and he kissed my lips, cheeks, eyelids and then I felt his tongue tease my mouth. My breath hitched and I thought I was going to fall over but he held me up.

The house moaned and groaned and yet there was no wind; behind the door, Argo and Agnes barked furiously.

Jack pulled away. "Are you alone?" he looked over my shoulder.

I nodded trying to get my head back in the now. "Uncle Seb is still away and Adam hasn't returned from a friend's."

"Shall we go then?" he asked. He handed me the roses.

"They are beautiful, thank you. My first bouquet," I told him.

"Really?" His eyes lit up. "I thought you would have received many by now. Well, I'm honoured," he bowed slightly. "You know, white roses mean new beginnings and the long stem means I will remember you, always."

I inhaled them and drank in their beauty and meaning. "Thank you."

"The pleasure is all mine," he said, gazing at me intensely.

"I didn't know whether to bring a picnic or not but I've brought ..."

Jack shook his head. "I have it covered."

I nodded. "Well, thanks again then. If you wait outside for me, I'll let the dogs out of the lounge room and join you in a minute. I'll put the roses in water too."

He stepped outside and I reluctantly closed the door, scared he would disappear. I let Argo and Agnes out and they sniffed around me concerned. I assured them all was okay and gave them the run of the house. I raced to the kitchen, searched for a vase and of course Uncle Seb didn't have one! I found a glass ice bucket and filled it with water. The roses looked rather grand in it.

I returned to the front door, patted the dogs once more and then the door wouldn't open. I looked skyward.

"Please house, I promise I'll be okay," I said. The house moaned again louder than before and then relented. The door loosened and I slipped out, closing it behind me. Jack stood a little down the path waiting for me. He watched me approach.

"You look ... there are no words for how beautiful you look," he said taking my hand.

I walked hand-in-hand with Jack, my skirt billowing around me, him in his dark suit and he led me across the road to our rock.

JACK

I had waited a century for a love like this and tonight I can't describe what it was like to know I am going to be with her, my soul mate. She was breathtaking, her eyes sparkling, their blue colour accentuated and reflected in her pale blue cardigan. Her hair and skirt moved around her like she was a spirit, I could barely control myself. I wanted to hold her, absorb her, crush her to me and become one, feel her around me; I have to own her.

"I'm sorry if you dressed to meet Uncle Seb and Adam and then they weren't home. Uncle Seb was supposed to come home this afternoon but he's staying a few more days at the conference," she said.

"I dressed for you and you only," I said. I waited as she leaned on me and slipped off her little ballet slippers. I pulled off my shoes and socks, rolled up my suit pants a few turns, grabbed the shoes and we entered the beach feeling the cool sand beneath our feet. I reached for her hand. She was nervous, I could feel the energy rippling through her.

"Are we going to our rock?" she asked. "Or are you going to show me where you live?"

I smiled. "I am going to show you where I live but not right now. I've been preparing it all week."

"Really," she said surprised.

"Yes. I was busy at work while letting you catch up on your sleep," I told her squeezing her hand. As we came towards our rock, I didn't lead her up it, this time we went behind it. There in a small enclave in the rock, sheltered from the ocean and the wind, I had set up a table for two.

She gasped with delight and looked up at me.

"It's perfect, Jack," she said. "The most perfect thing to ever happen to me."

I waved my hand over the table and the candles lit up.

She looked at me surprised.

"Is that a ghost talent?"

"Maybe," I teased. "I can't give away all my secrets."

The sea air was cool and I invited her to sit. I reached for her hand across the table. For what seemed the longest time we just stared at each other. I still felt strong but I had recharged all week almost.

"First course," I said.

"Yes?" she smiled.

"Touching."

I heard her sharp intake of breath and her heartbeat hammered.

OPHELIA

It was the most perfect night of my life. If anyone had told me I could ever be this happy, I would not have believed it.

We had a table for two in a hidden enclave in the most idyllic spot in the world and no-one else in the world existed except the two of us.

Jack took my hand and declared the first course was touching.

"Don't move," he said. He turned my palm over and barely touching me, he ran his fingers up my arm. I broke out in small goosebumps, the feeling was overwhelming. He continued to trace me and study me, moving along my shoulder, slowly up my neck and touching my lips. The whole time he watched me. I did all I could in my power to try and breathe normally and not fall into him and kiss him.

He traced my lips, moved up my cheek, across my brow and he

moved his hand down and closed my eyes. I heard myself inhale sharply.

"Second course," he said. "Kissing."

I kept my eyes closed as instructed and I felt him within a hair's breadth of my face. The chill around me gave him away and I knew if I leaned forward just a fraction I would touch his lips with mine but I waited in agony. He knew it and teased me mercilessly. His tongue touched my lips and I groaned with the pleasure and the pain of it. Then a little more, and a little more until his lips pressed against mine and we tasted each other. I could die now and be happy forever.

"You are too much for me Ophelia," he moaned.

I opened my eyes and looked into his deep blue eyes, as dark as the ocean.

"What are you saying, Jack?" I asked in fear. I couldn't breathe.

He shook his head.

All I could do was stare at him. I was scared to speak, scared to say the wrong thing, scared he was breaking up with me.

A few moments later, he whispered: "third course, dancing." Suddenly we were on the rock and Jack was holding me tightly, my hand in his; his other hand against my back pushing me against his chest. The waves rose and crashed on either side of us with ferocious power and the ocean looked so dark and foreboding that fear ran through my veins.

A waved thundered over us.

"Jack!" I called out.

"I have you, you're safe," he gripped me but all I could see and hear was the ocean on either side of us and the frightening roar of the waves. I clung to him, terrified.

"Do you want to see where I live?" he asked.

"We're going to be washed out to sea," I trembled as waves crashed above us and over us and all the time we stood in the middle, dry and cocooned, Jack calm and in control.

"Jack, please," I begged.

Jack swept me up and I gripped his jacket as if my life depended on it. In seconds we were back on the sand again, back near our romantic table. I was breathing fast.

"I've scared you," he said. "I'm sorry, I didn't mean to frighten you." He held me close and stroked my head.

"Not you, Jack, the ocean frightens me," I said, shaking.

He led me to a chair at our private table and lowered me into it. Jack knelt on one knee in front of me and took my hands.

"But I am the ocean, Lia," he said softly. "I'll take you home."

"No!" I protested, "I don't want to go home. All week I have lived for tonight, please, can we stay?" I pleaded.

"Only if your heart calms down," he said still holding my hands. He moved closer to hold me.

I pulled away and looked at him in surprise. "I can hear your heart beating."

"Of course," Jack said.

"But you're ..."

"Dead?" he filled in the word. "I can take the form just like you in every sense."

I leaned back and smiled at him. "But I'm not taking any form, this is me!" I reminded him. "So can you ... you know ... take another body?"

Jack shrugged. "Maybe. But this is me, I like my body. I'm a good looking guy," he grinned. "Why would I want to be someone else?"

I breathed out, a long sigh. "You are my beautiful guy." I looked into his eyes and thought myself the luckiest person in the world.

"And you, my beautiful Ophelia, are my life. Now that your heart has settled down nicely, please let me tempt you."

HOLLY

I nudged Harry when Jack escorted Ophelia to the dining table he had set up. How super romantic, I hoped something like that happened to me one day. Soon would be good.

"Let's go," I said and Harry nodded.

We headed the opposite way up the beach so they couldn't see us.

"Do you still think I'm crazy?" I asked Harry.

He dug his hands into his jeans' pockets and shook his head. "Okay, maybe not this time. I'm not saying I believe in that ghost crap, but he definitely seems to have some ... power."

" I can't believe he took Lia on the rock when the waves were pounding like that—they could have been washed away and she was freaking out."

"The waves weren't pounding anywhere else, did you notice?" Harry said. "Just on that rock and only when he went on it."

"I noticed. I'm worried for Lia," I said. "I think we should talk with Adam and tell him. Maybe we need to do one of those things where we confront her."

"An intervention," Harry said.

"That's it. But we might not have enough time either, we may have to let Ophelia know what and who Jack is before it is too late."

"You think she doesn't know?" Harry asked.

"I don't know," I said as we reached the beach path that led home. "I'll call Adam first thing in the morning."

OPHELIA

Jack stood up and returned to his chair opposite me. With a wave of his hand, he relit the candles and then, reached under the table and pulled out a little black cooler which I hadn't seen hidden against the rock.

"We have a 'love' menu," he teased.

I bit my lip, a little concerned and a little intrigued. He looked so handsome in his suit sitting opposite me that sometimes I forget to speak for staring so hard.

"Ophelia, are you with me?" he asked.

"I am," I promised him. "So, what is 'love' food and will we both be eating?"

"Of course, I have to keep up my strength. You're very wearing Ophelia," he gave me a wink. He pulled out a small, dainty covered glass dish, two small white butter plates and a large white plate, a container with two small silver forks and napkins, and two crystal water glasses and a bottle of water.

"Love food is luxurious food that entices the senses and the taste buds. I'm going to serve you a small sample of my favourites because it is all about the taste," he said. "Perhaps you would be good enough to pour the water?"

"Perhaps I will," I teased him, taking the bottle he opened for me and half-filling our glasses. "And when did you become a connoisseur of food?"

"I've had many years to refine my tastes and some good, um, teachers over the years," he explained.

My eyes widened. "You mean you have had lovers?"

"Ophelia! I'm 128 years old! I have had some company, especially from some wealthy older women. After the first war, times were particularly decadent." He cleared his throat. "But a gentleman never tells."

"But you are my first real boyfriend, my first kiss," I pouted but not seriously.

"And you are my first real love in all those years. You have no idea how long I have waited to feel this way."

As he spoke the moon broke free of the clouds and seemed to hang right over our table. A more perfect setting could not be painted. Jack opened the glass dish and using a set of small tongs he put the contents of the dish on the large white plate. It looked like such a delicate feast. Creamy blue cheese, oysters, strawberries, chocolate, figs and dainty biscuits and breads.

"First, the oyster," he said.

I grimaced.

Jack frowned. "I knew you would make that kind of a face ... as cute as it might be. Have you ever tried an oyster?"

"No, but they look so ... alive and slimy."

"They are sublime. Lia, everyone needs a teacher and I am yours," Jack said. "I could live on oysters. I love the texture, the taste; I even love the beautiful shell they are in."

"True," I studied them. "They have their own serving dish."

"Fresh from the ocean. You will find these particularly creamy. Now you must put it on your tongue, close your eyes and truly taste it," Jack instructed.

I nodded keen to please him. We both took our little silver forks and taking the delicate oyster from its shell, I placed it in my mouth. It wasn't as bad as I thought and I wanted Jack to think I had worldly tastes, so I closed my eyes, tasted its creaminess and swallowed. When I opened my eyes, Jack still had his eyes closed but he looked like he was in heaven. His eyes blinked open.

"Divine. You'll come to love them," he assured me. "This cheese is my favourite — blue and creamy." Again he studied me. "If it is too rich or not to your taste ..."

"No, I'm keen to try them all," I assured him. If his past relationships loved these sophisticated foods then so would I. Eventually. I accepted a small serve of the cheese on a plain slice of cracker. He wrapped the cheese up in its paper again.

"Close your eyes and truly taste it," he instructed.

We didn't get to the strawberries and chocolate for a while after that. He wanted to taste each of the dishes on my lips and on my tongue.

Later when Jack walked me home, I asked him to come in with me.

"Not to do anything serious yet ... you know ... but we could stay together," I said, stumbling over the words.

Jack kissed my hand and bowed. "We have all the time in the world Ophelia and when I lay beside you for our first night together, it will be on the large bed I have prepared for you and you will be my wife. You know I am an old-fashioned guy."

He stood full height, looked down at me and cupped my face. He kissed me again.

"Goodnight my Ophelia."

He stepped back and before I could form words, he was gone.

CHAPTER 26

OPHELIA

Sunday morning: I lay in bed just daydreaming. The sun was trying to stream in through the gaps in the curtain. I rose, pushed them back and looked out to sea—the tide was out and the surfers were a fair way out waiting for a wave. No ships were on the horizon. I dropped back into bed, fluffed up my pillows and lay under the quilt thinking of Jack. Life was so good, again. I wondered if he was thinking of me.

I can't wait to see his place and the room he has prepared for me. I can't wait to introduce him around too ... why not? If he can take a form and eat, why can't he be part of my life and his secret be our secret? I felt a cold chill and I whispered his name. Jack appeared; he leaned against the window frame, crossed his arms and grinned.

"Of course I'm thinking of you. All I do is think about you ... you are intoxicating," he said. And then he was beside me on the bed. "Even with bed hair!" he added.

Embarrassed I tried to flatten it down, but he grabbed my hands, pushed me back on the bed and pinned me down. I hadn't brushed my teeth and it was all I could think about. Jack didn't seem to care.

He moved closer to my lips, his eyes watching mine the whole time and then he pressed his lips against mine and kissed me.

"Good morning," he said.

"Good morning," I uttered as best I could.

"Would you care to see my home tonight?" he asked casually.

"Yes! Absolutely." He released my hands and I threw my arms around him.

"I've prepared every part of my house for you, for us. It is a school night though," he teased. "You probably should be in bed early Sunday night. We could leave it until next Friday night."

"No," I protested. "That will kill me. Tonight is perfect! I'll probably be the only one home anyway—Uncle Seb is still away and Adam will go out for sure."

"Then shall we say nightfall? Seven p.m. on our rock?"

"Perfect," I said reaching up for him to kiss me again but he was gone and I dropped back down on the bed. But I would see him tonight! My phone beeped with a message. I looked at the clock on the wall; it was just after nine a.m. and probably time I thought about getting up. I lazily rolled over and picked the phone up. It was from Holly.

Hey Lia, how was your date? Great I hope! Hx

I sent a message back; hard to write how brilliant it was in a few sentences.

"Brilliant. Seeing him again tonight, going to his place. I'm a goner. All good with you? Lx" I laid back and waited for the next beep. It came within a minute.

Got to finish assignment today. Ho hum. Hope to surface before midnight. See you tomorrow. Hx

I sent back some kisses, an offer to help if needed and debated getting up. I could daydream about Jack for just a bit longer.

HOLLY

"What will you do if Ophelia answers?" Harry asked as I went to dial Adam after texting Ophelia on Saturday morning.

"I'll hang up," I said, "and leave it a while. I wish I had his mobile number." I took a deep breath and dialled Ophelia's home number. "Pick up the phone, Adam, please pick up the phone." And he did!

"Don't say my name Adam, I need to speak with you," I said as soon as he answered 'hello'.

"Okay," he said.

"Sorry, it's Holly," I introduced myself.

"Hey there H..., how are you? Ophelia is upstairs if you want her?"

"No I need to talk with you, it's a matter of life and death, maybe, well could be."

"Uh huh," I heard him say.

I looked to Harry who was frowning at me.

"Adam, is there any chance you could drop in today sometime? Harry and I are worried about Lia and I have something to show you but you have to keep it to yourself," I said.

"Is everything okay?" he asked with concern in his voice.

"I hope so, could be nothing. Can you come?" I asked again.

"I'll be there in thirty minutes if that suits?" he said.

"Perfect, see you then." I hung up. Hopefully, the three of us could come up with a plan, if Adam believes me.

ADAM

High drama at the Harry and Holly household by the sounds of it. I took a quick shower before I headed down the road to their place. I hadn't heard Ophelia overhead yet, she must be lying in. I quickly dressed, topped up Argo and Agnes's water bowls and gave them a breakfast snack then grabbing my keys, I headed out. I left the car behind and headed down the driveway hoping Ophelia wouldn't spot me.

Before I knocked Harry opened the door, hit me on the back by way of a greeting and invited me in.

"Thank you, Adam, for coming," Holly said offering tea, coffee, juice and half the fridge. "Actually there's not much here," she stared into the fridge.

"Mum's out shopping," Harry explained.

Seated at the dining room table with coffee and a plate of stale Honey Jumbles in front of us, Holly pulled out her iPad and showed me some photos she took last night of Jack and Lia. Then she showed me the shipwreck photos of Jack and told me she believed Lia was dating a ghost. When she finished, I asked to see them all again. I told Harry to Google where Jack Denham was buried while I looked through the shots again.

"Warrnambool cemetery," he said after a few minutes. I sat back with a low whistle.

"It's out there, isn't it?" Holly sat.

"Way, way out there," I agreed.

"Too out there?" Holly asked.

I frowned. "You're talking to a guy with a family curse over his head and relatives who have died from being too near the water late at night. Wrong person to ask."

"Then we have to take it seriously," Harry said. "We need to let Ophelia know what we've found."

"But we've done that," Holly stepped in. "Peggy and I did that the other day and she thought it was hilarious."

I took my pullover off; it was getting hot or maybe it was the tension rising. I looked from Harry to Holly. "Okay, so she either does think it is hilarious or she knows and she's masking it. And looking at that vision last night, this guy Jack has put her in real danger."

Holly reached for her phone and swiped it; she showed me a message.

"So girly," I frowned, noting the kisses.

Holly rolled her eyes like I didn't have a romantic bone in my body; yeah, she might be right.

"Forget the kisses, Ophelia is meeting Jack again tonight. He's going to take her to his place. Does he have a place or is it the La Bella?" Holly asked.

Harry shuddered. "That's creepy."

"Sure is," I agreed with Harry. "I think we need to be on duty tonight. Where do they meet?"

"That rock that was in my video. They called it their rock, so I'm guessing that's the meeting point," Holly said. "You won't like this but ..."

"Mm ... what?" I asked suspiciously.

She looked at Harry for moral support.

"Well, I think given your family curse and given we might need all hands on deck ... sorry didn't mean to do a shipping pun ... we need to get Chayse and Peggy involved."

"No way," I shook my head.

Harry agreed about Peggy. "She won't be allowed out so count her out. But we can pick her brains if we need to and she's got big brains. But Holly's right Adam. If you're going to be there with us to try and stop Jack, then Chayse needs to be there to protect you from the curse or save you from it or delay it ... you know whatever it takes."

"He'll do it for Lia," Holly said. "So will you, won't you?"

She had me there.

"Okay, we meet here this afternoon to discuss our plan," I agreed.

"I'll contact Chayse," Harry said. "I'll text Tyler and get his number."

I rose to go. "Hey, thanks for letting me know Holly. But just one thing, I can't guarantee Chayse and I won't come to blows. You know, should Jack want to take him instead, well so be it," I smiled.

Holly smirked at me. "Seriously, you two have to get over it!" At least she had stopped making puppy dog eyes at me, for now anyway.

CHAPTER 27

OPHELIA

*A*dam was acting weird again, all day. I don't know whether he had gone another round with Vanessa or was just weird. He kept watching me and I was watching him and Argo and Agnes watched us both; they sensed something was going on. It would be good when Uncle Seb got back; I missed having the captain of the ship at home, so to speak.

As predicted Adam went out leaving me and the dogs alone until I was to meet Jack. He invited me along so I wasn't alone but then I decided to tell him I had a date with Jack. Oddly he didn't give me the third degree or a heap of warnings, he just asked what time and where we were meeting. He might be getting more trusting or he's got a big date and is distracted. Hopefully the latter.

I didn't know what to wear to see Jack's house but since my ethereal look was a hit last night, I thought I would go for something similar. This time, I dug out my long sleeve red crepe dress that fitted to my hips then ballooned out in a skirt that fell just below my knees. It was heavy enough to be warm but not too formal to look silly on the beach. I opted for some black ballet slippers which I could easily carry and I would take my black wrap.

Night was filling in the dusk. I had taken Argo and Agnes for a walk earlier and we met up with some of our regular dog friends. I fed them and they were happy to settle in for the night, while my chest was starting to ache with the anticipation of seeing Jack again.

HOLLY

Adam texted; Ophelia was meeting Jack at the beach at seven p.m. so we were there in position on the beach but out of sight at six-thirty. Our location was close enough that we could run and stop Jack hurting Ophelia but not too close to be seen. Imagine if we got it all wrong and we were spotted! How mortifying, plus Ophelia would never forgive us.

Harry was right, Peggy couldn't come but she had a few wild theories of her own. She thought Jack would take Ophelia with him underwater to his home. I doubted they would dive at night. I was thinking he might take her out on a boat above the waters where it lay, or sort of hover ... I'm guessing ghosts can do that sort of thing.

Just before seven, we saw her walking down the beach. She looked beautiful in red with her pale skin and dark hair.

"She looks hot," Chayse said and Adam nudged him in the ribs.

"What? She does!" Chayse defended himself.

"Yeah focus Romeo," Adam grumbled.

"I'm here aren't I?" Chayse said. "Even if it means spending my night with you."

"Yeah, must be hard to tear yourself away from the female population for the night but do your best."

Chayse went to reply and I cut them both off.

"Forget Jack," I said. "If you two can't play nicely together I'm going to knock you both out myself."

Harry grinned and Adam smiled sheepishly. Chayse looked shocked that I would say that to him; most girls just looked at him with adoration.

"Who is this Jack guy anyway?" Chayse asked, juggling the binoculars from Adam.

"He's a nobody," Harry said and laughed at his own joke. "Get it? A no-body?" We all looked at him and he stopped laughing.

"Right then," Harry said, "focus."

"Ophelia is almost at the rock, where is he?" Adam asked, taking the binoculars back from Chayse and scanning the beach.

And then Jack appeared from out of nowhere. It was freaky—he was just beside her like he had always been there which made me worry that he had been right behind us all the time, maybe. Ophelia must have sensed him or he had done this before because she showed no fear, just turned and threw her arms around him. Jack picked her up to kiss her and whirled her around. He did look pretty gorgeous; it was like watching a scene from a movie. I felt both Chayse and Adam bristle beside me.

Jack put Ophelia down and admired her—he made her twirl for him in her red dress, the skirt billowing out. No wonder Ophelia was taken, he was really dishy. He wore jeans with a white T-shirt and black coat. I guess he's learned a few fashion tricks over the years compared to that daggy sailor's uniform he was wearing in the photo. He took his jacket off, placed it on the sand and lowered Ophelia onto it. He sat down beside her.

"Great, how long are they going to talk for?" Harry complained.

"Could be hours," I said turning my back to them and dropping down into sitting position. We all relaxed and stood down, keeping our voices low so the wind wouldn't carry them over to the pair. It was a nice night; a clear, crisp night sky and a waning moon. I looked at the three guys around me—my brother and two of the most popular guys in the 'hood. If anyone had told me six months ago I would be at the beach with Chayse Johann and Adam Ferrier I would have thought they were insane.

Adam glanced at his watch.

"Worried about the curse?" Chayse bated him.

"Chayse, on my list of things to focus on tonight, the last thing I want to do is to have to knock you out," Adam said in a very controlled voice, "but it's still on my list."

Harry and I laughed and Chayse made a wry face in Adam's direction. We sat in silence for a while, just watching and waiting. Finally, Chayse spoke: "is it just me, or does the high tide look a little higher tonight than usual? It doesn't usually rise past that marker on the rock."

Adam turned to look, then looked skywards and out to sea.

"I think you're right, that's odd," he agreed. "So we're dealing with a stronger sea tonight too ... great."

Thirty minutes had passed and I began to wonder and worry if I had it all wrong. I would never live this down.

"On the move," Harry hissed and we all flipped around in haste. Jack was leading Ophelia to the rock and she was going willingly.

OPHELIA

Every time I am with Jack, I feel like we are the only two people in the world, and with absolutely no-one on the beach, it really felt like that. He wanted to show me his world and I couldn't wait. I don't know how he will do it—maybe we'll disappear together like he does all the time or he'll fly me there or we'll just float over the top—who knows, he won't tell me and says it is a surprise. A surprise I am about to experience!

We walked towards our rock. The waves were big again tonight but he promised me that I would be safe and we wouldn't have a repeat of last night's scare. I don't know how he could prevent the waves from breaking on the rock, but I'm going with it, trusting him. He went in front, extended his hand back to me and we walked up the rock.

Standing on the top was magic—in front of us lay our land; the sea and the moon at his command.

Jack turned to me and placed his hands on my hips. I looked up into his face.

"Are you ready?" he asked, brushing my hair from my face.

I nodded. I was excited and freaked out; goosebumps ran all over my skin and Jack rubbed my arms.

"We don't have to," he said. I could see the disappointment in his eyes.

"No way. I'm dying to see your place and the room you created for me," I assured him and I was. I just didn't like the water, it was so all-powerful.

He smiled. "Life's short, Ophelia, I know that better than most."

"As do I," I said thinking of the sixteen years I'd had with my parents. It seemed unfair that other people got a whole lifetime.

Jack continued: "So, I want to spend every moment with you, now and forever. As long as we get."

He dropped one of my hands and holding the other, took me right to the edge of the rock. He squeezed my hand. I waited for a vision or something to happen.

"Close your eyes my love," Jack whispered and I did.

ADAM

"They are seriously not going to dive into the water are they?" I asked.

"This is not good," Holly bristled beside me.

"I say we stop them now," Chayse started to rise and Holly pulled him back down.

"No just wait," she hissed. "Jack might be doing the scene from *Titanic* or something. You know, close your eyes and feel like you're the king of the world."

This time we all looked at Holly. She shrugged.

I subtly glanced at my watch again. I had plenty of time until midnight but I didn't want to tempt the curse.

"Don't worry about it, I've got your back," Chayse nudged me.

I looked at him trying to read if he was sincere or not. He would probably be the first to hold me underwater. I looked back to the rock. Jack and Ophelia looked amazing standing on the edge. The moon hung over the top of them and waves pounded against the rock. Ophelia's dark hair rose and fell with the ocean breeze, her skirt swirled gently around her and Jack stood tall, like he was in command and he was giving it all to her. It was my job to protect her, especially with Sebastian away but even being near the ocean at night was giving me the creeps.

And then the worst happened.

OPHELIA

I looked at Jack one more time; looked into his deep blue eyes and all I saw was love and desire. He smiled and nodded his encouragement. I tightened my grip on his hand and breathing in deeply; I turned to face the ocean and closed my eyes.

The falling.

The freezing water hitting me.

I tried to scream but water filled my lungs. I barely had time to realise that he had pulled me off the rock into the ocean with him.

I couldn't follow him; I couldn't breathe like he could.

It was so fast, so fast and the impact of the cold water on my face and body sent me into shock.

Jack was smiling at me; he was at home in the water, looking radiantly happy that I was with him, light coming off him and yet he didn't seem to realise I was dying.

I looked around in terror, the weight of my dress pulling me down. He wouldn't let go of my hand. I struggled to free it, to resurface for air but then Jack started diving down, deeper and deeper and taking me with him into the dark water.

～

HOLLY

I heard myself scream as I jumped to my feet. We ran—all of us ran to the rock. I couldn't believe what had just happened. She was there and then Jack went straight into the water so quickly and with such force and pulled Ophelia in.

Adam tore up the rock at breakneck speed and didn't stop on the edge; he dived straight in. I couldn't believe how brave he was. Chayse and Harry took the beach, pushing out through the waves. They were all strong swimmers but how far away would Ophelia be by now?

I stood on the rock looking out to sea for any movement. All I could see were the boys coming up for air and diving under again. I could hardly breathe for the fear coursing through me.

I began praying over and over, 'please don't take Ophelia from us, please bring her back, please bring her back.' Then I started praying for Harry's safety. We might spar a lot but he was my other half; I couldn't be without him.

Then I saw her.

She was much further out than where Adam, Chayse and Harry were diving. She appeared, floating on her back eerily lit by the moonlight.

Over the noise of the waves, I screamed as loud as I could to get Adam's attention when he came up for air and he turned to follow my directions. He began swimming towards her. I did the same when Harry and Chayse surfaced. Chayse followed Adam and Harry began to swim in. Tears streamed down my face, I didn't know if she was dead or alive but at least we had her. I ran down the rock as quickly as I could without losing my footing. I don't know how Adam tore up it so quickly before. I raced to get the towels and came back with them. I gave one to Harry who came ashore shivering and watched as Chayse and Adam swam in with Ophelia's limp form.

As they got into depths they could stand in, Adam carried Ophelia in while Chayse raced to me to get jackets and towels to warm her.

Adam placed her down on the towel; he and Chayse shrugged off the towels putting them over Ophelia instead. She was deathly pale. I hugged Harry and then released him. He didn't say anything, but he squeezed my hand reassuringly for a moment. I couldn't watch and I couldn't look away.

CHAPTER 28

OPHELIA

I don't remember much about the days that followed ... if a short or long time had passed. They said I had a fever and I lay in my bed waking every now and then to different faces and either the sunlight or moonlight peaking through the front windows. I glanced out at the sea sometimes and it looked calm, like a different sea to the night I was there.

I felt too weak to get up, but I tried a few times. I'm not sure how many days and nights passed but I felt disconnected from my body. Uncle Seb sat with me for hours, working away on his laptop in my room; sometimes I would wake up and Adam would be in the chair. He slept there for a few nights; I woke and watched him before drifting off myself. Harry came to visit and told me about his latest bike ride; Holly was there holding my hand and giving me advice in between complaining about Chayse; Chayse came and complained about Adam; and Peggy came and brought my homework. She said, "I know what you're thinking ... you don't want to fall too far behind." And this time she actually did know what I was thinking. My new friends were so important to me that I didn't want to repeat a year, I wanted to go into senior with them, so I did have to do some catch-up, soon.

Even Argo and Agnes leaned their beautiful heads on the bed quilt and watched and slept with me.

Jack never came. I never want to see him again.

ADAM

In her sleep, she called out for Jack and her parents—all the ghosts. I wanted to kill him. When Seb returned on hearing of Ophelia's accident, I told him the full story. Holly, Harry and I showed him the history, the press clippings and videos. He was more open to it than I thought but was angry at himself that he had been away. I think it brought back a lot of painful memories for him too.

Chayse and I even talked about what we could do to prevent Jack from coming back. We hadn't come up with anything yet but we both survived the talk—I guess that's something.

Ophelia has been bed-ridden now for four days but the doctor said she was fine to start moving around again, just in time for the weekend. She was pale and weak; the doctor said it was both physical and emotional. I think she was in love with Jack and now she's lost three people she loves in the space of a few months. I don't know where you go from there, but I'm here.

HOLLY

It's funny—Ophelia has only been part of our lives for such a short time but she's filled a big space. I don't know what I would have done had she not survived. I know I would have blamed myself for not acting quicker—when Chayse wanted to go in—but I guess we didn't know what was coming. Peggy thought Jack would pull her into the water but I thought that was ridiculous. What would I know? At least I raised the alarm in the first place, that's some consolation I guess.

One good thing that has come from it is that Chayse and Adam are actually speaking without knocking out each other's lights. Sebastian is really pleased about that too. And, wait for it ... Chayse sat and had a real conversation with me. Even bigger news—drum roll please and a bit of percussion—I was able to put words together and talk back. Yep, there's hope for me yet when it comes to hanging around Chayse Johann. Or maybe it was just because I was so distracted by what happened to Ophelia that I forgot to be speechless in his presence ... whatever.

I dropped in every day on my way home from school and this afternoon Ophelia moved over and I lay on the bed beside her. We talked about everything. She asked me how we knew and I told her about Peggy recognising his name on her assignment—I didn't say his name aloud—and how we checked out his photo and made the connection. She told me she really, really loved him. She still did but she didn't know he was going to try and drown her.

I suggested that maybe he was so in love and so keen to show her his world that he wanted to take her to the next world and that was just a necessary part of it. Jack thought she was open to it and understood the risk. We both thought about that for a while. Ophelia described the terror of hitting the water and I told her how Adam, Chayse and Harry ran to save her. She cried at the thought of the three of them risking their lives.

CHAPTER 29

OPHELIA

I can't believe how good they all are to me—Uncle Seb, Adam, Holly, Peggy, Harry and Chayse—I haven't done anything to deserve it but I am so grateful and touched. It blows me away. I tell them all the time, but they shrug it off, but I've learned to tell people how you feel in case you don't get another chance to do so.

Adam invited me to go for a dusk walk with him and the dogs on the beach and I accepted. It was weird; despite all that had happened, I still love the beach, the sand, the view and I couldn't wait to be back there inhaling the salt air. I wouldn't be going anyway near the water though except to walk in the firmer sand.

"Ready?" Adam asked reaching for his baseball cap on the peg near the front door. The dogs and I were already outside waiting.

"We're waiting on you," I told him with a look to the dogs. I shook my head and they agreed. Adam laughed.

"C'mon bossy." He took the dogs' leads from me and hung them over his shoulder on the towel already hanging there. We crossed the path and straight onto the beach. Magic.

The dogs expressed how I felt; happy to be free with our feet in the sand again.

Adam glanced my way. "Okay being here?" he asked.

"Sure, it's great actually," I said.

He nodded. Adam got it, it was in his blood. We walked along talking about nothing for a while. But I had to tell him ... I had to tell someone and Adam was my 'brother' and I trusted him. I can't believe the nights he slept in the chair near my bed until Uncle Seb came to check on me and roused him, sending him to bed. They didn't have to keep a vigil but they did.

I cleared my throat.

"Adam, I want to tell you something that happened, but I can only tell you if you promise me it will stay between us. I mean really promise me ... you can't tell Uncle Seb and swear him not to tell."

Adam looked at me. "Is it something I'm going to be able to keep to myself? You haven't seen him have you?"

I shook my head. "It's nothing like that but it is important, I think."

"Okay," Adam said. "I promise."

"No, I mean really promise because if you break this trust without me agreeing, I will never, ever trust you ever again," I said.

The dogs ran up to us, each one trotting around us with pleasure before taking off to chase each other again.

Adam crossed his heart. "Okay, I'll keep it in the vault but if it puts you in danger, then I'll be on your case to tell someone."

I smiled and offered him my hand to shake. Agreed.

ADAM

The kid is killing me. Now she wants me to swear to keep some secret ... after all that has happened, I can't imagine what's next! She offered her hand and we shook.

"Spill it," I directed her. She gazed up towards the lighthouse, drew a breath and bit her lip. I waited patiently.

"You remember how quickly we descended when Jack dived in and took me with him?" she asked.

I nodded. "Frighteningly quick. Chayse, Harry and I didn't have a chance. I saw you in the light that was coming from him; you were floating then you were heading deeper," I told her. "I thought you had drowned ... you gave me the fright of my life."

"Me too," she assured me. "There's probably no way that the three of you could have reached me or saved me. You were all really brave to try, especially you with the curse and everything," she said and studied me for a reaction.

"Chayse had my back," I admitted reluctantly.

"And Jack had all the power," she said.

"So, Lia, how did you get free?" I asked.

We all wanted to know this and what happened but the doctor said not to force her to talk in case it traumatised her. He figured she would tell one of us or a counsellor in due course.

"This is the secret I need you to keep," she said with a look around. "Jack wouldn't let go of my hand. I struggled and pulled but I don't know whether he was protecting me by not letting me go or trying to ... you know."

I nodded. I wasn't going to run the guy down, that would just make her defend him.

She continued. "When I had almost blacked out from no air ..." her hand went to her chest in fear as she said the words. I instinctively reached for her hand and took it. My large rough hand swallowed her small white hand but she held on tight.

"I saw ... it was Meg who saved me," she said in the quietest of voices.

I stopped and turned to face her.

"What? Meg ... Meg as in Sebastian's Meg?"

Ophelia nodded. "I saw some photos of her and I knew she

drowned, Uncle Seb told me. It was an accident but no-one knew what she was doing on the rock."

I drew a sharp breath. This was huge and I knew now why she didn't want me to say anything to anyone.

She tugged her hand away, looped it through my arm and pulled me to continue walking.

"It was Meg. Her hair was trailing all around her in the water and she looked so beautiful. She struggled with Jack and then others joined her. Other girls, all young and beautiful like they were preserved that way. But they weren't fighting him, it was Meg who pulled away with me, the other girls, they grabbed him as if they wanted him for themselves. Jack's face was distorted in anger, but I was only seeing bits and pieces, I was blacking out by then," she drew a breath.

"Meg had her arms around me and was pulling me to the surface, but I wasn't going to make it—my chest was bursting. Then she let me go and pushed me further upwards and I felt myself breaking free of the water and floating. That's all I remember."

My mind was racing; my heart rate was matching it. I tried to filter and sift through all the things she had just told me, like shuffling a deck of cards—all the scenarios.

"Adam," she said, "do you think Jack has ... you know ... drowned all those women?"

"Lia, did he ever threaten you?" I asked.

"Never. He was a total gentleman and we fell for each other. I could have walked away at any time, I'm sure."

I nodded.

"What are you thinking?" she asked.

"I don't know Jack, but I think from what you have told me that Jack has been looking for love, for the life he lost since he died. Each one of those girls he loved and wanted to be with; they wanted to be with him. It's just the consequences were fatal," I said.

Ophelia nodded. "But Meg, she wasn't under his spell, was she?"

I shrugged. "I don't know, I guess we never will. Maybe she felt she owed it to Uncle Seb to get you safely back. Maybe she regrets going with Jack, if that is what she did." I whistled to get the dogs' attention and we turned to walk back. "I don't know Lia," I exhaled. "Hell, this is freaky. Whether we believe Jack did that to the other women or not, we have to stop it. We have to make sure he can never come back—we can't take the risk that he could do that to you again or to anyone else, ever."

"He told me I was the love of a century," she said not making eye contact. "I wonder if he said that to everyone."

"No," I said. I didn't know but I wanted her to feel better about herself. "I think you captured him as much as he captured you."

She drank in my words, wanting to believe them.

"Those women," she started again, "their families don't know why they died. Uncle Seb said Meg was a good swimmer, he couldn't understand her death. Could she really have fallen for Jack?"

I frowned. "It's possible. I think Sebastian and Meg met at school didn't they?"

Ophelia nodded. "They were each other's first loves. Maybe that's why she got swept up ... she wondered what it was like to be with someone other than Uncle Seb."

"Sounds familiar," I said, thinking of Vanessa and trying not to sound bitter. "We could do some research and find out who the other women were ... see if you can recognise them."

She nodded. "Yes, there will be media clippings and photos of past drowning victims."

"Meg saved you," I said amazed.

"Saved by an angel," she smiled. "You will keep this between us, Adam, won't you? At least until I find a pattern to it all and I'm ready to tell Uncle Seb, and maybe Holly."

"Until *we* have some evidence," I said, with emphasis. "You're not in this alone, Lia. In fact, I don't want you doing any of this on your own. We'll research it together. Okay?"

"Okay," she nodded.

"It's just a bonus for you that you get the pleasure of my company," I added.

Caught off guard she laughed aloud and that was just the effect I was hoping for.

JACK

I saw her holding his hand on the beach. I don't know why she let go of mine. Sure, she was frightened and panicked but I told her I would look after her.

She hates me now, but she won't always. I'll wait.

I can wait, I have nothing but time on my side and I love her. I will love her forever.

THE END

Dear reader,

We hope you enjoyed reading *Ophelia Adrift*. Please take a moment to leave a review, even if it's a short one. Your opinion is important to us.

Discover more books by Helen Goltz at https://www.nextchapter. pub/authors/helen-goltz

Want to know when one of our books is free or discounted for Kindle? Join the newsletter at http://eepurl.com/bqqB3H

Best regards,

Helen Goltz and the Next Chapter Team

You might also like:
The Source by C.S. Luis

To read the first chapter for free, head to:
https://www.nextchapter.pub/books/the-source

Next in the series, *Ophelia Aground*

As Ophelia recovers she begins to form a deeper bond with Adam, but all that is about to change. Jack is waiting, planning his return to her if he can get past Adam and Chayse. Will the town's history of drownings be put to rest once and for all? And who are the unlikely couple who suddenly find themselves in love?

About Jack and the content of this book:

Ophelia Adrift is fiction; the story is derived from my imagination, but where locations, characters and incidents are based on experience, history or established locations, they are used fictiously. The fictitious character of Jack is named after a real person—the real Jack Denham or John Denholm as he is called in some historical records—but his traits and actions are created from my imagination.

I have used the real Norwegian-built barquentine *La Bella* and its crew as my muse. The *La Bella* ran aground in 1905 on what is now known as La Bella Reef, near the Warrnambool breakwater in Victoria, Australia. Of the twelve men aboard, five survived. The *La Bella* remains on La Bella Reef for divers to discover.

The story of the *La Bella* hero, William Ferrier is acknowledged in this novel and the accounts of the shipwreck are true as featured in historical records and news clippings from the era. Other characters while they may bear the name or surnames of the crew onboard the *La Bella*—Jack Denham, John Denholm, Chayse Johann and Adam Ferrier—their stories are fictional. The manner of the death of the book's protagonist, Jack Denham is accurate in keeping with the accounts of the shipwreck.

Jack Denham was buried on the 23 November 1905 at Warrnambool cemetery. However, there are discrepancies in archived newspaper records with some listing the La Bella ship's boy's name as John Denholm. Mr Clive Rayner, Secretary, Warrnambool Cemetery Trust advises there is a listing for John

Denholm buried on that same day, 23 November 1905 in an unmarked grave in the Church of England Section, Compartment 28, Grave 17. In all likelihood they are one in the same given it was 1905 and methods of record-keeping were subject to inconsistencies. My sincere thanks to Mr Rayner for his assistance in locating Jack Denham/John Denholm's grave. With my partner, fellow journalist, supporters of our 'Grave Tales' book series and Markwell & Swan Memorials, we have now placed a headstone on Jack's grave, more than one hundred years after his death at sea. The photo can be viewed at www.gravetales.com.au

I have taken great care to be respectful to any living descendants in the telling of this fictitious tale and despite the quirky theme, I hope it will highlight the beautiful south-western region of Victoria, Australia and its fascinating history.

ABOUT THE AUTHOR

After studying English Literature and Communications at universities in Queensland, Australia, Helen Goltz has worked as a journalist and marketer in print, TV, radio and public relations. She was born in Toowoomba and has made her home in Brisbane.

Visit her website at: www.helengoltz.com

Or Facebook at:
   www.facebook.com/HelenGoltz.Author

Follow on Twitter at: @helengoltz

The Mitchell Parker series (crime thriller):

Mastermind

An ambitious plan to switch two planes in mid-air began as an online game … but now it is more, much more. It is a plan to mastermind the perfect crime. Will Special Agent Mitchell Parker and his team discover the plot before it is too late? If you love it when a plan comes together, hold on, because nothing is about to go right!

Graveyard of the Atlantic

Below the surface of the ocean, off the shores of Cape Hatteras, lie the bodies of many ships that never made it to shore and something more … silent and sinister. It's a rough and violent ride for Mitchell Parker and his team against the ocean and the clock.

The Fourth Reich

The stilted footage of Holocaust survivors marching through the gates of Auschwitz projects behind Benjamin Hoefer at the book launch of his father, Eli's biography. As it comes to the end, four red words are scratched across the last frame— Nazi, Jew-hater, fake! FBI Special Agent Mitchell Parker and his team, find themselves in the middle of a neo-Nazi plot that spans two continents and threatens to bring one of the worst atrocities of history back to life.

NOTES

CHAPTER 13

1. http://www.standard.net.au/story/2327629/shipwreck-hero-william-ferrier-faced-local-animosity/

CHAPTER 14

1. LA BELLA WRECK. (1905, November 16). The Argus (Melbourne, Vic. : 1848 - 1957), p. 5. Retrieved February 26, 2015, from http://nla.gov.au/nla.news-article10035788
2. THE LA BELLA WRECK. (1905, November 24). Geelong Advertiser (Vic. : 1859 - 1924), p. 4. Retrieved February 26, 2015, from http://nla.gov.au/nla.news-article149122824
3. LA BELLA WRECK. (1905, December 29). The Colac Herald (Vic. : 1875 - 1918), p. 2. Retrieved February 26, 2015, from http://nla.gov.au/nla.news-article87609392

CHAPTER 15

1. THE LA BELLA WRECK. (1905, November 24). The Advertiser (Adelaide, SA : 1889 - 1931), p.
   4. Retrieved February 28, 2015, from http://nla.gov.au/nla.news-article4983143

CHAPTER 19

1. THE WRECK OF LA BELLA. (1905, November 22). The Sydney Mail and New South Wales Advertiser (NSW : 1871 - 1912), p. 1313. Retrieved March 1, 2015, from http://nla.gov.au/nla.news-article164998493
2. WRECK OF THE LA BELLA. (1905, November 18). Western Mail (Perth, WA : 1885 - 1954), p. 44. Retrieved March 1, 2015, from http://nla.gov.au/nla.news-article37809782

   Hamlet by William Shakespeare, published 1603. Quotes sourced from http://www.shakespeare-navigators.com/hamlet/H22.html

   References to John Denholm (instead of Jack Denham):

   WRECK OF THE LA BELLA. (1905, December 2). Observer (Adelaide,

SA : 1905 - 1931), p. 43. Retrieved March 4, 2015, from http://nla.gov.au/nla.news-article162444450

THE WRECK OF THE LA BELLA. (1905, November 24). *Daily Telegraph* (Launceston, Tas. : 1883 - 1928), p. 5. Retrieved March 4, 2015, from http://nla.gov.au/nla.news-article154018300

A Dictionary of Sea-Terms: http://navalmarinearchive.com/research/darcy_lever_glossary.htmlsourced from: Darcy Lever's "the Young Sea Officer's Sheet Anchor; or a Key to the Leading of Rigging, and to Practical Seamanship" with additions by George W. Blunt, New-York, E & G.W. Blunt, 1863.